…Karen lay curled against Mike, listening to him snore softly. She was almost giddy with excitement. Who would have thought? Claudia would have thought, she told herself. Oh, I don't know about that, she mentally argued back, reliving the lovemaking that had recently concluded. Well, she does call what she knows the *"keys to the kingdom"*…

Whether or not Claudia knew the power of what she had told Karen that day, Karen was more grateful, already, than she could have imagined. In place of the tears that she had become used to, a smile accompanied her to sleep.

"Until we transform the quality of relationships between men and women, we can't begin to resolve the issues we face in our world today. As a man, I pray that women everywhere read and take to heart this book. I also learned a great deal about myself. A must read for anyone interested in living a powerful life!"

—CARL ZAISS, International Business Consultant, Educator, and Author of *True Partnership – Revolutionary Thinking About Relating To Others*

Keys
to the
Kingdom

Alison A. Armstrong

PAX Programs Incorporated

Keys to the Kingdom

For information address:
PAX Programs Incorporated
P.O. Box 2107
Monrovia, Ca 91017

www.understandmen.com

Cover design: Bette Cowles-Friedlander
Cover illustration: Jeff Koegel

ISBN: 978-0-9741435-0-7

First edition published 2003

10 9

Printed in the United States of America

Acknowledgments

My HEARTFELT AND DEEPEST APPRECIATION TO THE FOLLOWING people without whom this book and my life's work would not exist outside of me: To Greg, my husband, for your love and my life. To Jeff, Claire, and Annie, my children, for the sweet inspiration of your wisdom, curiosity, support, hugs, and laughter. To Jeff Armstrong, my brother, for your love and support, and the joy your family brings me. To Sharon Todd, my mother, for your devotion and encouragement, always. To Dave Armstrong, my father, the adventurer, for your love and laughter and pleasure in life. To Lindsey, my sister, for the light you bring our family. To Mercer Carlin, my best friend, for your passion and love. To Don and Martha Lewis, the best in-laws imaginable, for your support, encouragement, and appreciation. To Rolland Todd, the Coach, for your support. To Joan McClain, PAX's co-founder and the first to believe, for your years of work to bring "the keys" to thousands. To S.R. Gabriel, for your joy, love, and guidance. To Barbara George, for your love, support, and leadership. To W.E., for your insights and encouragement, and the message that one person can make a difference. To Ellen Hurst, for setting me free from fourteen years of being afraid of men. To Denise Lynn, the angels' angel, for all your support and partnership. To Lisa Sasevich, my friend and colleague, for making it possible by holding down the fort with your passion and dedication. To the staff of PAX, my pillars, for your love and support and darn hard work. To Jolene Shepard, for your guidance and support when the pelican has me. To PAX's investors, for your generosity and support. To all the graduates of Celebrating Men, Satisfying Women,® my students, for your gifts and your lessons. To all the men who have taught me, for showing me yourselves, and thereby giving me the keys to a new world.

Introduction

by Alison Armstrong

THIS BOOK IS A LABOR OF LOVE FOR GRADUATES OF THE CELEBRATING Men, Satisfying Women® workshop and all people hungry for information and insights into joyful, satisfying relationships between men and women.

While our workshops create an environment and process for women to learn how to understand and appreciate men, and how to communicate with men in their language, *Keys to the Kingdom* exists to entertain as it enlightens and educates. The characters, while they may seem out of the ordinary, are based on thousands of real men and women who have learned and used this information since 1995. They have shown me that the topics within are surprisingly simple to use and profoundly alter relationships between spouses, lovers, friends, co-workers, parents, and their children.

I have had the luxury of learning about men over a long, leisurely twelve years, and continue learning to this day. I encourage the reader to pause, to reflect, to absorb, and to use each of the keys to the kingdom available in this tale. If you prefer a more linear, structured process for making sense of men and their behaviors, with plenty of diagrams and lists and exercises, please see the back of this book, or www.understandmen.com, for information about our workshops and other products.

Dedicated to

Clara Stockton Armstrong

❧

Always

The Covenant

As Claudia left her doctor's office, she politely said good-bye without her usual warmth or cheerfulness. Her carefully maintained sense of balance had been profoundly disturbed. In place of contentment, she felt doom.

She had gone to see if there was something her doctor could provide for her arthritis, which had been increasingly painful. Surprisingly, the family physician had recommended yoga instead of more medication. She thought it would be a good compliment to Claudia's avid gardening by slowly stretching the joints and muscles she didn't normally use.

Claudia's sense of dread was not a result of contending with the pain of her swollen and twisted joints. Rather, it was due to the other tests the doctor had performed, which indicated a notable reduction in her general state of health. This was not a surprise to Claudia, who had recently celebrated her seventy-seventh birthday.

When Burt returned from the lumberyard, he saw Claudia seated in her garden. This was not unusual; but the expression on her face and her slumped posture immediately caught his attention. She looked like she had the weight of the world on her shoulders. Burt felt his stomach lurch and went through the French doors in a hurry. He approached his beloved wife and asked gently, "Honey, are you okay?"

As Claudia looked up, he could see the tracks of tears on her cheeks. Burt couldn't conceal his anxiety. "Did it not go well at the doctor's? Is something wrong with the kids?"

Claudia gave him a small smile, obviously trying to ease her husband's concern. "Do you want to know the whole story, or the end first?"

Starting to breathe again, he settled himself on the seat across from her. "Start with the end and then tell me the rest."

He could tell that Claudia expected that response. After almost sixty years together, he was an open book to his wife, best friend, and lover.

"I'm supposed to go to yoga classes."

Burt's brows drew together, "And that's why you have been crying?"

"No." She took a deep breath and stated simply, "The tears are because I am *afraid of dying*."

Now Burt was really confused. He knew his wife was no more afraid of dying than she was afraid of a yoga class. Sure he must be missing something, he said, "That doesn't sound like you. You have never been afraid of dying before. Is there something the doctor told you that made it sound…imminent?"

Claudia replied, matter-of-factly, "Only the usual stuff. I am old and getting older. The gadgets say my blood pressure is a little higher, my heart a little weaker, my kidneys a little slower."

Burt kept listening, waiting for the rest.

She continued, more seriously, "But you're right. I am not afraid of *me* dying. I am afraid of *it* dying with me. And today I realized I don't have all the time in the world to prevent it."

Now Burt understood completely, having had this conversation before. The first time was when their daughter, Myra, turned sixteen, but without the fanfare that reaching that age usually generated in Claudia's family. It happened again when their only granddaughter, Kimberlee, turned sixteen, also uneventfully. Then again when Kimberlee got married and, most painfully, when she got divorced. Burt had been trying to solve this problem for his wife for forty years with no success; he felt disheartened being reminded of it.

But because he loved her more than life, he steeled himself for another attempt. "Okay, sweetheart," he began. "Maybe this time you'll let me help you." That seemed to catch Claudia's attention, and she looked at him quizzically.

He continued, "I understand, better than any man alive, that the women in your family possess some extraordinary and esoteric knowledge about men. I also understand that you have passed it only from mother to daughter for the last nine generations because of something called 'the Covenant.' But you have never explained the Covenant to me. If you did, perhaps I could help you find a way around it."

He could see Claudia hesitate. He knew she had not explained her family's covenant to him for a reason. He suspected it was because she wanted to honor it, not find a way around it. She had resisted when the temptation had been greatest—when their granddaughter had suffered the pain of her divorce. But this was worse even than that. He could tell she felt tortured by the idea that she could die with all her hard-won and precious knowledge. While this information had given him an extraordinary life, he knew that from her point of view, being the end of her line was like chopping down a rare tree before it bore its exquisite fruit.

She began slowly, "Okay, Burt, I will tell you. But I don't want to find a way *around* the Covenant. I want to find a way to work *within* the Covenant, if that is possible."

She added with sincerity, "Since you are talented at creating beauty with both the grain and the knots of your wood, perhaps you can find a way to work with this."

Burt swelled a bit with her appreciation, her praise inspiring him, fueling his determination to help her. Everything else disappeared as he focused entirely on what Claudia was now, finally, going to reveal.

Claudia began in a solemn tone, "As you already know, the women in my family began studying men back in feudal times, about five hundred years ago. The first was my great-grandmother, times twenty-three, Hesperia Keys. She began noticing profound differences in how men and women did things. Hesperia passed these observations on to her daughter, and challenged her to keep learning about men. She in turn was to pass it to one of her daughters, and so on. Over time, the women of the Keys family began to glean a deep understanding of men.

"Naturally, as they continued to grow in their understanding of men, they became highly effective in dealing with men. After several generations, other women began to notice that the Keys women received better treatment than they did. They were envious and wanted to learn the secrets to the admiration and generosity they were witnessing. Being kind people, the Keys began revealing their insights. At first, sharing the knowledge resulted in only good, but then something terrible happened."

Claudia's forehead knotted as she continued on, "Throughout human history, women have needed men to survive. We would literally have suffered and died without the protection and providence of men. Having that dependent relationship didn't bring out the best in everyone. It made many women extremely manipulative toward men—always trying to find a way to gain power and control over their physically and economically stronger mates. So, when my ancestors taught women how to bring out the best in men, these women naturally used their new understanding to become better manipulators.

"This horrified my great-grandmothers. From truly understanding men, they had come to admire and respect men instead of fear them. They learned how to communicate their needs to men, who responded magnificently. They thought men were incredibly generous people. What my great-grandmothers had learned made it possible for them to work in loving partnership with men.

"The idea that a woman needed to manipulate a man to get what she needed had long disappeared among my people. That the information would be used for anything other than the benefit of both men and women was unthinkable, until they saw it happen."

Claudia clasped her hands together in her lap. "That was how the Covenant was born. There were so many failed attempts to teach women outside the Keys family, that it was finally agreed never to try again."

Burt interrupted, "But how come the women in your family didn't use the information against men? Until very recently, women still needed men to survive."

Claudia smiled, a twinkle appearing in her eyes. "I think for two important reasons. First, each child grew up observing how her mother treated her father, and how she interacted with the other men in the family and in the town. She saw how her mother spoke to them and how they responded. From birth, each female child witnessed working partnerships between men and women. She also saw the ways in which her mother was powerful. She saw that, as much as her mother needed her father, he needed her as much or more, for different reasons. Between the two, the young women in my family never experienced the sense of powerlessness or weakness that drives women to manipulate men."

Burt smiled to himself. This explanation of the Covenant was revealing the source of the strength he had always admired in his wife.

Claudia continued, "This is why the Covenant includes an agreement never to skip a generation by teaching a granddaughter, unless the grandmother actually raises her grandchild. If a daughter doesn't have the experiential knowledge, then a granddaughter would not have grown up with the appropriate interactions with men. This is why when Myra refused her inheritance, I was prohibited from giving the knowledge directly to Kimberlee."

Burt was impressed. "I had no idea the Covenant had such a history."

Claudia sighed. "Now you can see why I am loathe to break it. I understand why it exists—to protect both men and women."

Burt was surprised. "What do you mean by 'both men and women'? I thought it only protected men *from* women."

"When women understand men, they are automatically more effective at whatever they do with men, including manipulating them," she said. "But manipulating men never works in the long run—it causes anger and alienation and interferes with the wonderful way men naturally relate to women. It always backfires, leaving the woman with less power, less credibility, and less support from men. Therefore, by *not* giving the information to women who won't use it in a sustainable way—in a partnership—the Covenant protects both men *and* women."

For the millionth time, Burt thought Claudia was amazing. He also thought he might have found the key to solving her problem. "Honey, maybe that's it. Find a woman who *would* use the information in a partnership with a man, and teach her what you know."

Claudia tilted her head to the side as she considered his idea. Straightening again, she said, "I am sure some of my great-grandmothers thought the same thing about the women they tried to teach. It is not always easy to recognize when a woman treats men as adversaries. In many women, it comes out under stress—like when they are not getting what they need."

She was pursing her lips in the way that tickled him; he loved her little mannerisms. She concluded, "But it is a good idea, honey. I will think about it. Maybe there is a way to choose a worthy student."

She sighed again, but it seemed to Burt that the weight on her shoulders was a little lighter.

Mike was in Africa, driving a Range Rover, surrounded by wildlife. Immersed partly in memory, partly in fantasy, he felt calm and happy for a moment. But then the freeway traffic slowed abruptly, pulling his truck and his exotic daydream up short. The calmness and happiness disappeared, replaced by a familiar anxiety and frustration.

Mike was making his way home to Pasadena from a work site on the west side of Los Angeles. Another remodel, another job well done. But where was the satisfaction he used to feel? Everywhere he looked, the things that used to give him pleasure, didn't. The things that used to fill him with pride, left him unimpressed. The things that had grabbed and held his attention, no longer interested him.

What mattered, anyhow? What was the *point*? Was *anything* important, really? And, *where the hell did these questions come from?*

Mike was afraid he was losing his mind. Was this a mid-life crisis? Was this what people poked fun at? Was this the thing that caused grown men to buy fast cars and date much younger women?

These thoughts had become familiar, starting out of the blue about eight months earlier. Everything had been going great. He had been accomplishing his goals with his construction business, finally getting it to run well without his constant attention. He was reaching his financial goals and looking forward to traveling again. He had started golfing and was enjoying more time with his cars and his friends. His relationship with his wife was comfortable and satisfying. He had felt so close to "it," to finally arriving at the long-sought destination of the last twelve years.

Then suddenly, his confidence had been replaced by uncertainty. His satisfaction turned to frustration and anxiety. The future, which had been clear and settled, was now completely up for grabs. Worse yet, he felt like "Mike" was up for grabs. He had no idea who he was anymore.

Mike had tried on several occasions to express these thoughts to Karen. At best, it was uncomfortable. More often, the conversations were disastrous. She was threatened by his questioning. He could feel her grasping for the life they had planned. She kept telling him who he was, the man she had known since college. Over and over she reminded him of all they had built together and how important it was. The more she said, the more isolated he felt.

Mike didn't feel like the man she had known for twenty years. He couldn't find that man. He wore that man's clothes, but they no longer felt right. Nothing felt right and he had no idea what to do about it.

Mike pulled into the driveway and parked his truck. When he entered the house, Karen paused from cooking dinner. She greeted him with a kiss on the cheek, but without the warmth Mike would have liked to receive from her. He could tell from the tension in her face and body that she was still edgy from the argument they had had the night before.

Mike went upstairs to their bedroom and changed his clothes, removing his work-shirt and pants and putting on his favorite shorts and UCLA t-shirt. He picked up a car magazine and sat down to leaf through it. About thirty minutes later, he went downstairs to the kitchen, where Karen was still making dinner. Forcing cheerfulness, he said, "Hi. How was your day?"

As Karen answered, he could tell she was striving for lightness as well. "It was fine. How was yours?"

Mike replied just as lightly, "Fine. Anything new?"

"I'm making reservations for Mammoth in December with the McConnells. Do you want to stay the same place as last year?"

Mike felt uncomfortable, quickly replying, "I'm not sure I want to go at all."

Karen's hand paused in mid-stir. She seemed surprised. "But we go every year!"

Mike growled, "Just because we've always done something doesn't mean we should keep doing it."

Karen was clearly restraining herself. "But I thought it was important to you. You've never questioned it before."

Mike felt frustrated. Why was this so hard? "I'm not sure if it's important. I'm not sure if *anything's* important. I just don't know if I want to go."

Now Karen was obviously irritated. "O.K., then I'll cancel with the McConnells and we'll do something else."

Something snapped in Mike and he responded angrily, "Don't do that! I didn't say we *weren't* going."

He could see that Karen was really riled up. She demanded, "So are we going or *not?*"

Mike shouted back, "I don't know! Quit trying to pin me down!" He stomped out of the kitchen and back up the stairs.

As Mike left the room, Karen felt the energy drain from her body. She took dinner off the stove and turned off the burners. She sat down at the kitchen table, put her head in her hands, and wept.

The argument was not a surprise. It had been happening nearly every day for eight months. Wiping her tears, Karen got up from the table, grabbed her gym bag from under the stairs, and left.

By the time she arrived at the yoga center, she was breathing normally again. Karen was grateful for her yoga classes; they were one of the few places she had been able to find peace lately.

As she entered the class, she noted a new student: a petite, older woman with short, wavy white hair, bright blue eyes, and soft, attractive features. There was something about her that immediately lifted Karen's spirits. She experienced a recognition that she couldn't explain intellectually but knew intuitively.

During the class, Karen observed the new student out of the corner of her eye. Through the instructor's interactions, she learned that her name was Claudia. Karen could tell that Claudia was new to yoga, but while unskilled, she followed the instructor's directions carefully.

At the end of class, Karen departed more slowly than normal, hoping to interact with the new student. As Claudia came up beside her, Karen greeted her cautiously. She was surprised by the warmth with which Claudia responded. It was as if the older woman had expected Karen's attempt to connect with her.

Claudia said in a pleasant, lilting voice, "I'm new to this group. Would you like to have coffee with me?"

Karen laughed at the incongruity of the calm-inducing yoga class being followed by a strong jolt of caffeine. But she responded enthusiastically, "I would like that very much!"

As their eyes met, a light, tingly feeling went up Karen's spine. They walked to a nearby coffeehouse, and Claudia accepted Karen's offer to treat.

Settling down in a quiet corner with their beverages, Claudia asked, "Your name is Karen, right?"

"Yes. Karen Trevino. And you're Claudia, right?"

"Yes. Claudia Lambert."

For a moment, the two women just looked at each other. Then Claudia said gently, "Tell me about yourself, dear."

Karen began slowly and politely, telling Claudia about her life. She intended to exchange the usual pleasantries of age, occupation, marital status, number of years in southern California, and so on.

But as Claudia listened to her with that kind, soft face and curious twinkling blue eyes, Karen's real life began tumbling out. "Mike and I met in college. He was three years ahead of me, studying business administration while I was getting a degree in early childhood education. We both had a sense of adventure and a desire to contribute, and we fell deeply in love. When he graduated, we married and stayed near the college until I finished. We played house and Mike held many different jobs, including several in construction."

Claudia nodded and Karen was encouraged to continue. "After my graduation, we joined the Peace Corps and spent several years in remote villages in Africa, mostly in Zimbabwe. We were a good fit for the Peace Corps. With Mike's construction skills and my love of children, we both had valuable contributions to make. During that time, I admired his stamina and his commitment. And, along with the satisfaction of our jobs, we loved the travel and excitement of the Peace Corps."

Karen sipped her coffee and noted that Claudia waited patiently. She resumed, "When I was twenty-seven and Mike thirty, we returned to the United States and began to get serious about our careers. I became an elementary school teacher and Mike started his construction company. We both put in long hours, Mike especially. He works hard to give us both a good life."

Karen paused and Claudia asked, "Do you have any children?"

Karen tried to hide her regret. "No, none of our own." She added, "But each year I gain a new crop of second graders." She explained, "Mike and I spent all of our thirties working hard and developing our careers. About a year ago, we started having a lot more fun again. Mike was working less; he seemed less driven. He was interested in traveling again, and we began making plans. I was excited about our future. It seemed like we were finally going to enjoy all we had created together."

At that point, Karen couldn't continue without revealing some of her bubbling emotions; she couldn't meet Claudia's gaze. She was both surprised and relieved to be revealing this much. But Claudia was so compassionate, and Karen felt safe and accepted.

She stared into her coffee cup and said sadly, "In the last eight months, Mike has changed a lot. He's moody. He's distant. It seems like if we talk, we fight." She paused, "I miss the fun…I miss the friend-ship…I miss *Mike*." Her throat closed involuntarily. "I don't know if we're going to make it. I know that too many couples divorce at this point, and I'm afraid that's going to happen to us."

Claudia reached across the table and gently patted Karen's hand. Karen noticed Claudia's gnarled fingers and swollen knuckles and guessed they were part of the reason she came to yoga.

Claudia said softly, "I'm sorry for your troubles, dear. I wish there was something I could do to help."

Karen nodded.

After a pause, Claudia asked, "How was your marriage before this? Would you say you had a good relationship?"

Karen perked up a bit. "Yes, I think we had a great relationship. We had fun together. We enjoyed each other's sense of humor. I supported him in building his business; he supported me in my teaching. I think we've learned a lot about each other over the last twenty years. And, I think I'm sensitive to his needs, even though I don't share them. We were good together. I thought we were going to be together forever."

"What do you mean by sensitive to his needs?" Claudia asked. "Can you give me an example?"

Suddenly, it seemed that her answer to this question was impor-tant to Claudia. Karen thought she must be mistaken, but something about the tilt of Claudia's head and a new intensity in her face seemed significant.

Karen replied, "Well, when I come home from work, I walk in the door and start doing what there is to do. I begin making dinner, I listen to the messages and check the mail. When Mike gets home from work, it's like his body's home, but he's not there yet. If I start talking to him right away, he gets antsy and doesn't seem interested in anything I have to say, even if I'm talking about something he normally cares about."

Since Claudia looked interested, she continued, "In the beginning, it bothered me a lot. I thought he didn't care about me or my day. But after a while I figured out that he needs something I don't need; he needs to adjust or something. Like he needs time to get used to being home."

She finished matter-of-factly, "So now when he gets home from work, I stop what I'm doing and greet him. Then I leave him alone for a while. It's funny, but every day he does the same thing, without fail. He changes his clothes; he reads a magazine or watches TV for awhile; and then he comes to me. I can always tell then that he's ready for me; that he's ready for *us*."

Worried that she hadn't answered Claudia's question well, she asked, "Does that make sense?"

Karen couldn't interpret the small smile on Claudia's face. It was as if she was satisfied in some important way, but Karen couldn't imagine how what she said could have that effect.

"Yes, it makes perfect sense, dear."

After a silence, Claudia said, "I need to go now, but I think we should do this again. Perhaps even have lunch or something on the weekend."

Karen was warmed by this invitation. She had become enchanted by Claudia in the short time they had spent together. It wasn't until she was driving home, thinking about what she would tell Mike about her, that she realized Claudia had said very few words. Karen knew next to nothing about this charming woman who had so simply entered her life.

As Claudia drove home, she thought to herself, "Gee, if Karen had only *one* key…if she only knew about the Stages of Development, she would have a chance!"

While her body was relaxed from the yoga movements, Claudia's mind raced with the possibilities. The small hope that Burt had given her just that day was growing with each new idea.

Burt looked up from his newspaper and instantly recognized the change in Claudia's posture. He realized how worried he had been by the relief he felt now. He set his paper aside and teased, "Wow, did one yoga class do all that for you?"

Claudia's eyes crinkled as a smile lit up her face and dimpled her cheeks. "Burt, I think I've found the one!"

He loved it when she smiled like that. "But I thought *I* was 'the One,'" he teased.

Claudia reached down to stroke his cheek with her small, arthritic, garden-worn hands. "Of course you are 'the One,' honey. You are the love of my life." She looked down at him eagerly. "But I am talking about the other one—the one that you spoke about today. The woman who could use my information in a partnership."

Burt's eyes widened in surprise. "Really? Just like that? How do you know?"

Burt listened as Claudia told him about her conversation with Karen. "Honey, you know when you meet someone and you have a chill of recognition? This woman, Karen—there's something so familiar about her. If reincarnation is true, I'd swear I knew her from a former life. Do you know what I mean?"

He nodded, "Yes, I know what you mean. It's happened to me." He paused. "I'm not sure if it's because I've known the person before, or if there's just something about them that I am attracted to that makes me feel like I need to know them. Like when I met you." He reached over and took her hand.

"Yes, like that! It was as if our hearts recognized each other." Claudia paused and lifted his hand to her cheek. But he could tell she was too excited to slow down for his reminiscing.

She let go of his hand and began gesturing. "A similar thing happened with Karen when she first looked me in the eye. And then as she told me about herself, I got goose bumps. It was as if the woman we spoke about today in the abstract was now magically sitting in front of me!"

Burt smiled at her enthusiasm. "What makes you think that she's the one?"

Claudia sat down. "Well, there was the way she talked about her husband, with some admiration. As badly as things have been going for them lately, she didn't speak ill of him. She seemed sad and lost, but not overly angry or bitter or complaining about what has been happening. This has me suspect that she doesn't think of her husband as an adversary."

She continued, "Then the clincher was when she told me about his Transition Time."

That was a term Burt wasn't familiar with. "Transition Time? What do you mean?"

"It's something the Keys women learned about men a long time ago that Karen figured out on her own. This tells me that she may really want to understand her husband."

"But what is Transition Time?" asked Burt.

"Transition Time is that period of twenty or thirty minutes that men need to adjust to being at home. During that period of time, men usually do the same things. And it's remarkable how similar those things are. Men often change their clothes. They might check the mail or check their messages. They might get something to drink or a snack. They might turn on the television. Many read a paper or flip through a magazine. They rarely want to talk to anyone."

Claudia became more animated as she spoke of her knowledge. He wondered why she didn't talk about it more often.

"Transition Time can involve a lot of different things, but there's a ritual that a man goes through to shift from what he's been doing out in the world to being at home. Now that's just one example. Men actually have many Transition Rituals that they use to shift from one thing that they're paying attention to, to the next thing they're paying attention to. And they use these rituals throughout the day—at work, home, everywhere—to shift their focus."

He understood. "Oh, I know what you mean. You call that Transition Time? But why is there a name for it? Doesn't everybody do that?"

Claudia shook her head. "Well, no, not everybody. It's not something normally needed by women, because we think differently. Women pay attention to more than one thing at a time and they shift easily from one thing to another. Unless they're doing something very masculine for a long period of time. Then they'll need Transition Time, too."

"Now why is it significant that Karen learned this about her husband?"

Claudia replied, "It's significant because most women assume that when a man comes home from work, he's ready to interact with her, and she begins asking him questions, or sharing about her day, or getting him involved with something right away. And if he seems agitated by this, she usually takes it personally and thinks that he doesn't care about her or about the family, or she thinks he isn't glad to be home."

She grew solemn as she continued, "Usually her reaction to it is negative. She blames him for not doing what she thinks he should do, or being the way she thinks he should be when he gets home. A couple might fight about this same thing over and over again. Or a woman might get her feelings hurt over and over again and withdraw."

"That's too bad."

Claudia added, "But that's not all. After the man has completed his transition, he's ready to interact with her and probably wants to be with her. But because her feelings are hurt, she's angry with him and cold, which he doesn't understand. It creates this whole cycle of distance and hurt and disappointment."

She sighed. "Most women never figure out that men are just different and they need Transition Time. If you give men their Transition Time, at the end of it they'll be glad to participate with you, especially if you're friendly and happy to see them. It's a big part of what they came home for."

Burt nodded. "Of course it is." Encouraging her to go on, he asked, "So if a man needs Transition Time, what should a woman do?"

"Well, she should do what Karen's been doing, which is why I'm delighted by her. She should treat him as an important person when he arrives home and show that she's glad to see him. She should stop what she's doing to greet him well. He's important enough to deserve that.

"And then she should leave him alone. He'll come back when he's ready. She needs to trust that. She needs to trust that he wants to be with her, and after he's adjusted, he'll come. Until then, she can do what she wants to do."

She added, "Of course, if she wants to spend time with him, she shouldn't seem too involved in something when he comes back. If she is, he'll probably leave her alone out of courtesy."

Burt agreed. "That's certainly true for me. Since I hate being interrupted, I assume that you do, too."

Claudia smiled at him affectionately.

"So what are you thinking of doing with Karen, if she is the one?"

Claudia paused for a moment. "I'm not sure yet. I need to think about it a lot more. I'm almost certain that I'm going to depart from the Covenant in some way. But I need to think about how I'll start. I want to be careful and honor the spirit of it, even while I'm taking chances."

Burt smiled. "I can't wait to hear what you come up with."

Claudia gave him a grin that made her look years younger. "Well, knowing me, my mind will be working on this even while I try to sleep. Ask me again in the morning, okay?"

Burt smiled again, got up from his chair, and helped Claudia up from the couch. He put his arm around his wife's shoulder and said, "Alright, I will."

As they made their way to their bedroom, he kept his arm around her and turned off the lights with his other hand. Dressing for bed, he knew that he'd be getting a lot more sleep than Claudia tonight.

Mike heard Karen's car pull into the driveway and his heart beat a little more rapidly. He went downstairs to meet her as she entered through the garage and stood in her way, cautiously putting his arms around her. He felt her stiffen and then relax, and finally, felt her hug him back.

He leaned down, pressing his face into her soft black hair, and breathed deeply. He whispered, "I'm sorry."

"I'm sorry, too," he heard Karen reply, with her face resting in the pocket between his shoulder and chest.

Mike enjoyed this moment of peace, feeling the old familiar warmth of their relationship. He wondered how long it would last.

Burt wasn't surprised that Claudia slept in. He had awoken about midnight and was almost positive he could hear her thinking. Noticing her dressing now in their bedroom, he put on water for tea, popped an English muffin into the toaster, and waited with anticipation.

After her enthusiasm last night, Burt was optimistic about Claudia's dilemma for the first time in many years. Mostly, he had watched her suffer. He often thought of Claudia's rheumatoid arthritis as a physical representation of the torment she felt. The symptoms seemed to have started not long after she realized that Myra would continue to refuse the information that was her inheritance.

As long as Myra refused, the Covenant prohibited Claudia from helping Kimberlee. After hearing the reasoning behind the Covenant, Burt could see now that in their daughter's disinterest, Claudia felt doomed. Since he usually viewed life from his passion for wood and woodworking, Burt thought of Claudia being prevented from passing on her knowledge in those terms. It seemed that being stymied by Myra created knots in Claudia's spirit just as the arthritis knotted up her hands.

Burt hoped that her solution for helping her yoga friend would include some way to help their granddaughter, too. This could give Claudia the relief she needed.

When Claudia entered the kitchen, he could tell that all traces of uncertainty were gone. Her sense of doom had disappeared and she was alive with purpose. Her soft, full cheeks glowed and her eyes sparkled even more intensely than usual. She kissed him on the cheek, then chose her tea from a variety in the cupboard and fixed it in the cup Burt had set out for her. She buttered the English muffin and settled down in the adjacent booth where they took most of their meals. She was obviously enjoying the warm sunshine as it came through the south facing kitchen windows and further brightened the pale yellow room.

Burt poured his coffee, added cream, and seated himself across from her, as he had almost every day since his retirement. His eyes gazed warmly at the face he had loved for so long, enjoying this moment on the edge of her new adventure. Finally, he said, "I'm ready when you are. I can't wait to hear what you've come up with."

After a sip of her tea, Claudia began. "As I told you yesterday, the Covenant was created to protect men and women because it seemed impossible to have women outside of our family learn this information and use it in partnership with men."

Burt nodded.

"But there is something my ancestors could not have anticipated. In creating the Covenant, they assumed that women would always need men to survive. Technology leveled the playing field. Physical strength no longer matters the most. But my ancestors had no way of knowing that a combination of technology, World War II, feminism, and more reliable birth control methods would change everything for women. My great-grandmothers couldn't have foreseen a time when women would no longer depend upon men to merely survive."

Burt nodded again, encouraging her in the way she liked.

Claudia continued, "I am hoping these changes will make it possible for women to have partnerships with men, without the precedent of hundreds of years of experience that I have in my family. Again, we had no way of anticipating this and there's nothing in the Covenant to deal with it. But I think my great-grandmothers would all want me to take advantage of this new opportunity. Some of them would approach it more recklessly than I. Others, more cautiously. But I think what I intend to do is consistent with the spirit of the Covenant."

Impressed but not surprised by her integrity, Burt asked, "And what is it you intend to do, my love?"

"I intend to teach Karen about the Stages of Development."

Hoping she would talk to him like she had last night, Burt asked, "What are the Stages of Development?"

"The Stages of Development explain the ways in which men change, in steps, you could say, from birth to seniority. They explain how these changes affect how men approach all different aspects of their life—their work, their friendships, their relationships, and their family. It explains the differences between men in various stages, and will help Karen to deal with what's happening to her husband right now."

"Sounds fascinating! Will you teach me, too?"

Claudia giggled, sounding youthful. "It seems funny to teach a man about being a man. Especially since I am used to learning *from* men, not the other way around. But it sounds like fun." She teased, "Maybe I can work that in."

Burt smiled, delighted that he had made his wife giggle. "Why did you pick the Stages of Development? I am assuming you know a lot of other things, too."

"Yes, I do know more—much, much more. But I picked the Stages for two reasons. First, because it will help her with what is happening to her husband. Second, because if I'm wrong about her, it would be difficult for her to hurt Mike or other men in her life with that particular information."

Burt was curious. "What do you mean? Some information is more dangerous than others?"

"Definitely. There are some things about men that, if used improperly, can cause a great deal of harm."

They sat in silence for a while. Burt noticed the way the sunshine reflected off Claudia's short, wavy white hair. He was as enchanted as when it had reflected off her long, wavy brown hair.

Burt asked, "So you really think Karen is the one?"

Claudia smiled. "Are you reading my mind? Actually, I am thinking Karen might be the *first* one. I might start with her as an experiment to see if women are ready for this information. If it goes well with Karen, perhaps she could share the information with others. She is a teacher, you know."

"Will you tell her that you think she might teach others?"

"I don't think so. I think I'll see how she responds to the information itself, and if she has a natural desire to help other people with it."

"Is there anything else that you've decided?" Burt asked.

Claudia's eyes flickered, clearly delighted by how well Burt knew her. "Well, this is a small start, but you know how determined I can be, and I refuse to die being the only one who knows what I know."

Burt nodded, hearing the challenge Claudia had given herself, and glad that she had found a way to begin.

Karen was disappointed when she didn't see Claudia at yoga class on Tuesday night. She kicked herself for not asking for her phone number. When she arrived at class on Wednesday, and saw Claudia there in her pale pink leotard and modest sweatpants, Karen was surprised at the relief she felt. She waved to Claudia and felt happy when Claudia smiled back warmly.

At the end of class, Karen waited for Claudia and they left the building together. Karen was disappointed again when Claudia said she couldn't stay for coffee that night. Unwilling to let go, Karen asked, "Do you still want to have that lunch we talked about?"

Claudia looked down and smiled to herself in that way that made Karen wonder what she was thinking. She looked up and said, "I would love to do that. When?"

"How about this weekend?"

"Wonderful," Claudia said. "Would you like to come to my house?"

Karen didn't want to impose. "How about we meet at the coffee house?"

To her surprise, Claudia replied, "I'd actually like some place much more private."

Karen's eyes widened. "Private?"

Claudia looked at her seriously, meeting her gaze. Karen unconsciously held her breath. "Remember the other night, when I said that I wished I could help you?"

Karen nodded. Claudia continued, "Well, I can."

Somehow, Karen knew that Claudia wasn't talking about the usual bunch of advice she'd been getting from her friends. Letting out the breath she had been holding, Karen said, "Okay. I would like that very much."

Claudia handed Karen a card with her name, address, and phone number on it. Karen noticed that she'd taken it from her pocket, as if she were ready for this encounter.

"How about Saturday at noon?"

Karen could only nod, her mind beginning to spin as she wondered with excitement what this unusual woman had to offer. Spontaneously, Karen quickly hugged Claudia good-bye and was surprised to feel Claudia return the embrace.

The Beginning

As Claudia prepared for lunch with Karen, she thought of all the things she could teach her. Mentally, she divided the information into categories. First, there were topics she thought were directly relevant to Karen's situation. Second, there was information she thought would provide great benefit. Third, there were things that she was open to telling Karen, but didn't know if she would. Finally, there were topics she thought too risky to teach someone outside of the lineage.

Claudia felt stronger physically, buoyed by her new sense of purpose. She hoped intensely that what she was about to begin would be fruitful and give her a way to help Karen and her husband. Secretly, she wished that through helping Karen, she would find a way to reach Kimberlee, her beloved granddaughter.

She silently said a prayer, finished preparing lunch and, expecting it to be needed, began setting aside an afternoon snack.

After lunch, Karen and Claudia settled in at an unusual table overlooking Claudia's beautiful garden. Karen could not have told anyone the details of what she had just eaten, nor recounted the small talk that accompanied their meal. She could not have described Claudia's home or even told someone its color. But nearly every word Claudia spoke after that point, Karen remembered.

Karen noticed a change in Claudia. She still had the soft, attractive features, with a wide smile and deep dimples, high cheekbones and bright blue, twinkling eyes. But now there was a certainty and a resolve that Karen had not seen a mere five days ago. Karen sensed that this change in Claudia had something to do with her, but she could not imagine why.

Claudia began, curiously, by telling Karen her name again. She said, "Karen, my full name is Claudia Keys Mitchell Lambert. Lambert is my married name. Mitchell is my maiden name. Keys is my middle name."

She continued with emphasis, "*Keys* is the middle name given to every girl child in my family. It is usually explained simply as a family name. But when a young woman turns sixteen, she finds out that "Keys" refers to 'Keys to the Kingdom'. She is told she was given it as a middle name to remind her always of the importance of her inheritance."

She paused. Karen could see Claudia watching her face to see how what she had said was being heard. Although skeptical about the "keys to the kingdom" part, Karen kept her expression open and interested. Apparently satisfied with what she saw, Claudia continued, "As I grew up, I heard bits of information about men and women being different. Just little things here and there. Most of what I first learned was from watching my mother and my grandmother interact with my father, uncles, brothers and cousins. How they behaved didn't seem unusual until I got a bit older. Then, as a teenager, I spent some time at my girl-friends' houses, and saw how their mothers interacted with their brothers and their dads. I was surprised. So when I was about fifteen, I began to suspect that my family wasn't quite normal."

Claudia took a sip of her tea with her little finger quaintly crooked to the side. It reminded Karen that Claudia must be in her sixties. She became a little nervous that she was going to hear her entire life story.

"When I turned sixteen, a special ceremony took place with my mother and my grandmother. As part of that ceremony, they explained to me about our ancestors. I found out then that the women in my family had been studying men for more than five hundred years. Like me, each daughter found out about this when she turned sixteen. At that point, if she chose it, she was given the task of learning what her mother and grandmother knew, confirming that knowledge in her own experience, and then adding to that body of knowledge with her own research."

Karen's eyes must have shown her surprise, because Claudia paused and tilted her head to the side in a question. Karen, speechless, nodded for her to continue.

"In turn, she passed it down to her own daughters. By luck, all these years there has been a daughter who wanted to pursue the research. By now, after twenty-five generations, the quantity of knowledge is immense. Since full-time study was not possible, it took me nearly fifteen years to learn what my grandmother had been given. Another five years passed as I learned what my mother had added. Then it took many, many years to validate it all with my own experience. It's only been in the last twenty years that I've begun my own investigations."

Karen was in awe. She had never heard of anybody doing such a thing. But she was puzzled, too. "I'm fascinated by what you are saying. Forgive me, though—I keep wondering why you are telling *me* these things. You mentioned earlier that you have a daughter and grand-daughter, right?"

A shadow of sadness passed across Claudia's lovely eyes. She answered quietly, "Yes, that's true, I have both a daughter and a grand-daughter. But, when the time came, my daughter did not choose to follow in my footsteps." Tears suddenly appeared in Claudia's eyes and began to flow down her cheeks. She wiped them away without trying to conceal the emotion.

Karen waited while Claudia composed herself. "When I met you," Claudia said, "I had been concerned that I would die not having passed on any of this information. After some thought, I made a decision. If you're interested and willing, I will teach you some of what I know. I will give you some of the keys to the kingdom."

Karen could feel Claudia studying her face as she assimilated what she had just been told. She was interested, but skeptical and cautious. Hoping she didn't sound unappreciative, she replied tentatively, "No offense, but women are so different now than they were five hundred years ago, even a hundred years ago. Do you think that what you have to teach me would be relevant today?"

To Karen's relief, Claudia didn't seem offended. Instead, Claudia smiled as she responded, "I appreciate your honesty. I can see how you might think that, because of my age, I would teach you something out of Ozzie and Harriet, or worse, the Victorian era. I assure you that even though my knowledge goes back twenty-five generations, it is revolutionary today." Claudia held Karen's gaze. "You're probably wondering why I would say that." Karen nodded.

"For thousands of years, women have depended upon men for their very survival. Because of this need, women have manipulated men to get them, to keep them, and to get them to do what they wanted. But the women in my family have long regarded men as partners to be supported and encouraged and appreciated. The information we have gathered has helped us to do that very effectively, making both our lives and their lives easier and more satisfying.

"One of the reasons that I have decided to share our knowledge with you is because times have changed in a way that wasn't anticipated. Now, because of feminism and technology, and yes, birth control methods, women are able to provide for themselves and to protect themselves like never before. I am hoping that these changes, this progress, makes it possible for women, specifically *you*, to hear and use what we have learned in the way it was intended: to create potent, fulfilling, equal partnerships between men and women."

Karen quietly absorbed what Claudia was saying, her eyes sweeping the garden but barely seeing all the flowers in late bloom. Claudia sat calmly and waited. Karen remembered the books she had read about women in earlier times. How few options they had, even as recently as fifty years ago. She remembered her grandmother's dependency upon her grandfather. At the time, she thought it was her grandmother's weakness. Now she could see that her grandmother had fulfilled what was open to women at the time. Karen could also see that she took her own independence and self-sufficiency for granted. She immediately made the connection that where there is dependency, equal partnerships are not possible.

Karen tried to recall any couples that she considered to be good partners. As scenes from her memory flickered through her mind's eye, she saw that, for the most part, women still manipulated men. That even seemed normal. Now she understood why Claudia said her approach, while not new, was revolutionary.

Karen said, "I can see that what you're saying is true for me and everyone I know. I can see that my ability to take care of myself creates an opportunity in my relationship with Mike to be partners. But I have no idea how to go about it. I have only learned how to be careful and time things just right, and how to get what I want by being angry or upset or coy."

Claudia was clearly warming to her subject, and her hands began to move as she talked. "In the normal relationship women have with men, women are adversarial toward men. They treat men, often, like enemies. Most women don't even realize they are doing this. It includes employing many different methods to make men weak. I am inviting you to learn from me because I think to some degree you have escaped this. By adapting to Mike's need to adjust after work, you have already demonstrated a desire to support him instead of making him weaker."

Karen was surprised and immediately realized she should not have been. She had known that Claudia was paying close attention to what she said and how she said it. "It's true; I do want to support him. And I thought I was pretty good at it…But lately, nothing I do works. Can you help me with that?"

Claudia leaned forward a bit in her chair. "Yes, I can. But first, let me explain to you the approach my family has taken. Then I will tell you what you can expect from our spending time together and what I would expect from you. It will be up to you to decide."

Karen agreed. Claudia said, "There is a notion among people that we exercise free will all day long, with little acknowledgement that we are members of the animal kingdom. Just like every other species, we have ways of behaving that are not by individual choice at all, but rather, are characteristic of our species and done by instinct. I call this aspect of people 'the human animal.' There are also significant gender differences among most species. Besides human animal characteristics, we have specific male and female characteristics. In addition to understanding ourselves as humans, by understanding ourselves as male and female we can be more effective with each other. The women in my family have been studying the differences and similarities between the male and female human animal."

Claudia took a sip of tea. "Since the beginning, our discoveries have challenged our assumptions, revealed the depth of our misunder-standing, and finally, provided illumination."

Karen was barely breathing. With every new concept that Claudia presented, she grew more excited. What kind of wealth had she stumbled upon? But she spoke her concern, "Are you saying there are no individual differences?"

"Of course there are, dear. Think about it like ice cream. Do you like ice cream? What flavors of ice cream do you like?"

Karen said, "I like pralines and cream, and mint chocolate chip."

Claudia smiled. "Perfect. There are a lot of differences between those two flavors, aren't there? And among all the others you can find at the grocery store?"

Karen nodded. Claudia said, "Think of the differences in flavors of ice cream as the differences between individual men. Men come in a wide variety of flavors."

Karen thought to herself, Yea, some with nuts and some without! She tried to keep a straight face but her nostrils flared, revealing her amusement at her own joke.

Claudia continued and Karen hoped she hadn't noticed. "We are going to talk about men, not at the level of flavor, but at the level of ice cream. No matter what flavor it is, it still has the properties of ice cream, yes? It still freezes and melts the same. You could apply that to men if you like."

Karen wondered, Can she read minds, too? Keeping such a straight face that Karen wondered if she had misread her, Claudia went on, "What I will teach you, should we come to an agreement, are char-acteristics of men that determine their behavior, which they cannot change. If you use what you learn, you can save yourself a lot of heartache. And it will be just like understanding how your car works or being able to speak the language in a foreign country. You'll be able to get more of what you need with less effort and less frustration for both you and your husband."

Karen responded excitedly, "I've done many things over the years to improve my relationship with Mike. Some of them have worked, most of them have not. But it sounds like what you're talking about is different from anything I've tried before. It sounds different from anything anyone has tried before."

Claudia replied, "I think most women try to improve their relationships with men either by changing themselves or attempting to change men. I think we both know what happens when you try to change men. It doesn't turn out well. And we are bombarded with messages in television and magazines, and from our friends, that if we change ourselves to become what we think men want, then men will treat us the way we want. Women are usually trying to be more of something, or less of something, to fit the ideal they think men are looking for."

Claudia sighed. "If women changed how they understood men, and then by that understanding, how they interacted with men, they would be much more effective. And changing our understanding and our interactions is much easier than changing ourselves."

Now Karen was leaning forward in her seat. "I can see what you're saying. I thought if I were less intelligent, Mike would be more confident and take charge in our relationship. I thought if I were quiet and mysterious, he would be chasing after me instead of me chasing after him. Could it be that they have nothing to do with each other?"

Claudia smiled a knowing smile.

"Wow. This could be great news!" Karen said, feeling hopeful. Then she became anxious. "You said that you would tell me what you expected of *me*. I'm a little nervous about what that might be. Is now a good time to tell me?"

Claudia leaned back in her chair and took another sip of her tea. Karen felt her heart begin to beat faster.

"There are several things that I require. First, that you're honest with me. Second, that what we begin, we finish. Third, that you keep our conversations confidential, with the exception of telling your husband. Do you agree?"

Karen nodded slowly, a bit relieved, and asked, "What are the others?"

Claudia leaned forward, her eyes holding Karen's, showing the full force of her will. She said slowly, enunciating each word, "You must promise never to knowingly use this knowledge to hurt, diminish or disempower men in any way. You must promise never to willfully invalidate yourself for not already knowing this. And you must promise to forgive yourself, in advance and as necessary, for any mistakes you find out you made."

Karen gulped. She sensed intuitively that these last requirements would affect her life in ways that she couldn't yet imagine. First taking a sip of her tea, not noticing that it had grown cold, she said, "I...agree."

Claudia leaned toward her again and asked, "And do you *promise*"?"

Karen almost laughed at Claudia's thoroughness. Taking the leap, with as much conviction as she could muster, she said, "I *promise*."

Burt had worked with wood since his father taught him to whittle when he was six. He had spent many summer and winter days turning odd bits of wood he'd found into animals and human faces. Woodworking in many forms had given him an interesting and useful hobby as he grew up. As a young man, whittling had provided hours of solace during his stint in the war. Afterwards, he had made a career as a carpenter. As a father, his whittling had earned the admiration of his young children, and since his retirement, carving figures and making furniture had provided hours of peaceful contemplation. A major bonus of his hobby was the way his creations made Claudia happy.

Burt was now busy sanding the 1x3s that would become the seat of the bench he was making. It was a surprise for Claudia that he had been planning for many years, but had been too tired to pursue. Claudia's newfound purpose had energized him and today he approached his new project with relish.

Mostly while he worked the wood, he thought about nothing. Claudia had told him long ago that the ability to think about nothing was characteristic of men and one that, as a woman, she envied. But today, as he sanded each seat board to a buttery soft finish, he wondered how Claudia and Karen were getting along. As serene as Claudia could be under any circumstances, he knew that today held a great deal of importance for her. He hoped that Karen would be everything and more that his wife needed.

He wanted the bench he was making to provide another place for Karen and Claudia to sit during their upcoming discussions. Burt was assuming that Karen would accept Claudia's invitation and the conditions that applied. She would be a fool not to, he thought. If she could take what she learns from Claudia, and make her husband's life a fraction as fine as Claudia had made his, he knew her husband would worship her.

Publicly, Burt's buddies—all old men now—had teased him for his obvious adoration of Claudia. Privately, each of them had asked him what their secret was. He had always replied, "I think it's Claudia. I'm just an ordinary man. I try my best to make her happy, and, bless her, she lets me." Invariably, the buddy would nod his head, understanding perfectly how much that meant. Burt had always felt a little sorry for his friends that their wives didn't understand them as Claudia understood him.

If all goes well today, he thought, this guy Mike is sure to be a lucky fellow.

Burt went to his workbench to get an even finer grade of sandpaper. Looking out the window, he gauged the time by measuring the angle of the sun in the sky, as was his habit from the Navy. As he did, he noticed Claudia seated with Karen at the dark wood table he had made her years ago. Claudia was speaking and Burt could read the intensity in her gestures. He hadn't seen her that animated with another person in a long time. He returned to his sanding with a smile and a glint in his dark eyes.

Not forgetting her duties as a hostess, Claudia thought it was time to refresh themselves before going too far into the lesson she had planned for today. She and Karen went to the kitchen for a fresh cup of tea.

As they prepared their tea, Karen asked Claudia about the future. "I know I already agreed 'to finish what we start.' What do you have in mind and how long do you think it will take?"

Claudia replied, "We should be flexible, since I have never attempted this before. But, I think we should meet like this for two to three hours, once a week, for about a month."

Karen seemed surprised. "Really? I thought it would take a lot longer to teach me all you've learned about men."

Claudia chuckled. "It would take years to teach you all that I know about men. But I am only planning to teach you what you need to know and can really use considering what is happening with Mike right now."

Karen seemed impressed. "Wow. You sound like a doctor; like you know what to prescribe for what ails me."

"If used properly," Claudia said, "what I teach you can be like laser surgery. It will remove the tumor growing in your marriage, without scarring."

She watched Karen take this in. Claudia was impressed that, usually, Karen thought before she spoke. She could see her absorbing what Claudia told her, tasting it, rolling it around in her head, before she reacted. This was a good sign. So far, she's teachable, Claudia thought. She chuckled to herself and wondered what Karen would think about her pronouncing a teacher "teachable"?

They gathered their tea and the small plate of cookies Claudia had prepared earlier and returned to their places in the garden. Claudia was having fun—it felt good to talk about what she knew. It felt good knowing she could help this young woman. She decided to start with the familiar and build from there.

She said, "Since you are an elementary school teacher, I am assuming that you studied child development in college or have since then."

Karen responded enthusiastically, "Yes. I have my degree in child development."

"Perfect. As you know, children develop in predictable stages, acquiring new abilities at certain times. And while some children enter a stage earlier or later than others, they all go through them. Right?"

Karen nodded. "Yes. Many parents think it says something about their children's abilities if they go through a stage ahead or behind other children. They'll brag about it if their child enters a stage early."

Claudia nodded in understanding. "Most people are not aware that in addition to child development there is also what we call 'man development.' Men continue to develop in predictable stages from infancy through seniority, with changing motivations, needs and capacities that affect every part of their lives."

Seeing that Karen was right with her, Claudia asked, "Are you familiar with the idea of animals being imprinted? For example, a baby zebra's brain being imprinted with the image of its mother's stripes to enable it to find her from then on? Or baby birds thinking the first creature that they see is their mother?"

Karen nodded. "Does that apply to people, too?"

Claudia smiled. "I believe it does. I believe we are 'imprinted' with the first man that we have an intense experience of in our teens. It may be a young man in a romantic situation. From then on, we think that all men are like him. We spend our adult lives waiting for the forty-year-old to do what the seventeen-year-old did. Or, for some of us, it is our fathers who make the impression, and then we can't understand why younger men don't act like him."

"I can see what you're saying," Karen said. "I'm not sure which one it was for me. I'll have to think about that."

Claudia continued, "We don't normally recognize or understand the tremendous differences between men in different stages. Because of that, we treat all men the same. This has us expect things that men can't provide, and not know how to deal with the behaviors that are natural for each stage. Over the next few weeks, we're going to talk about the four stages my family has become aware of, plus one very different state that occurs for some men. Understanding the Stages of Development is one of the keys to the kingdom."

Claudia paused and looked at Karen. This time, she saw less resistance to the words "keys to the kingdom."

"First, let me say something about the names of each stage. Since we began studying men in feudal times, what we've named each stage came from the terms that applied back then. I think you will find that they still make sense today."

Karen asked, "Do you mind if I take notes?"

"No, that's fine, dear," Claudia said. "In fact, I recommend it."

Claudia waited patiently while Karen extracted a pen and a spiral-bound pad of paper from her purse, and turned to a blank page.

Claudia began, "We're going to start with the second stage and then backtrack. As you'll see, it is easier to understand this way."

She continued, "This is the stage that we call Knight, as in Knight in Shining Armor. This stage begins at puberty and continues into the late twenties or early thirties. Think of a Knight in shining armor: can you see what his life is characterized by? His life is about adventure. The Knight is very passionate. He lives his life in the present—now, now, now. Being challenged and having fun are extremely important at this stage."

Claudia paused, "Can you see what I'm saying so far?"

Karen nodded, "Yes, I can. When Mike and I first got together in college, having fun and sharing adventures was all we thought about. I think I was ready to settle down a long time before he was."

Claudia thought this was going well. It was good to see Karen immediately applying the information to Mike. Later on, Claudia could encourage her to apply the information to other men in her life.

Claudia continued, "Many of us have had our hearts broken by a Knight or two. This is because a Knight may really love a woman passionately, even have chosen her and think of her as his future wife. But often he's not ready to get married when she is. This is because for a Knight to *settle down* means literally to stop having adventures. It means putting away his sword and selling his horse."

She smiled compassionately. "It sounds like the end of life as he knows it and loves it. Knights will often respond to talks about marriage with, 'But I haven't done everything I want to do.' They may still marry young, especially if that happens in their culture, but usually with the attitude that marriage is the next adventure."

Claudia saw the light go on for Karen, who said, "That must be what happened with Mike and me. Mike's family is old-school Italian. Marriage is something expected in his family in their early twenties. But getting married had nothing to do with settling down. We had already made plans to join the Peace Corps when I graduated. And while Mike waited for me to finish my degree, he held a lot of odd jobs. Usually when he quit one, the reason he gave was that it wasn't any fun. Or that it was boring."

Claudia said, "Can you see how it works? The need for fun and adventure is extremely strong at this stage. You must have been a lot of fun and adventuresome yourself for Mike to have married you."

As Karen replied, Claudia noticed a bit of sadness in her voice. She said, "Yes, I was a lot of fun back then. I laughed a lot and enjoyed doing new things. I've become serious. I wonder why."

Claudia warned her, "Karen, this is the first time, but it won't be the last. It is natural to invalidate yourself by what you see. But everything I'm going to teach you is in order that you can make choices about how you want to be. So that you can be the person you want to be on purpose. Becoming serious and forgetting to have fun is normal for women beginning in their thirties. That is important for you to understand now. Later on, if you want to do something about it, I'll tell you what to pay attention to."

"Thank you," Karen said, "I'm sorry I interrupted. Please tell me more about Knights."

Claudia resumed, "If a Knight becomes a father, he often will feel that it is making him become responsible before he's ready. It is a burden he will likely resist and may complain about. A Knight's attitude toward his children is usually in looking to have fun with them. You will hear them say things like, 'He's five months old now and a lot more fun.' Children respond to their father's sense of play and behave differently than they do with their mothers."

Karen commented, "Mike kept saying that he wasn't ready for children. I didn't understand that. I can see that I didn't realize that he meant he wasn't ready to be responsible for them. That they might have gotten in the way of the fun and adventures we were having."

Claudia replied, "Good. This is the beginning of having more understanding of what it's like to be Mike." She continued, "One of the most important things to understand about Knights is that men are always some part Knight. Even King Arthur put on his armor from time to time. In other words, men always need challenges and adventure. How much challenge and adventure a man needs is something important to learn about an individual man. Younger men tend to seek challenge in both their jobs and their recreation. For some men, as they grow older, they get all the adventure they need from their jobs or from their recreation. Burt is challenged each time he decides to create another piece of furniture for me. He's challenged by how beautiful he can make it, how comfortable he can make it, and how long he can keep the surprise."

Claudia smiled to herself, as she thought of Burt in his shop right now. "The mistake we make is thinking that their need for challenge is an immaturity or misbehavior on their part. It is important to understand that it is part of their nature. A woman who tries to stand between her man and his adventure is in trouble. She'll be regarded as a kind of enemy to what he needs."

Claudia watched as Karen processed this information. She could see her thoughts in her golden brown eyes. It was one thing to think about Mike in the past. Now, she was thinking about Mike in the present.

"I'm not sure how much adventure Mike needs now," Karen said slowly, "or where he gets it. I've never even thought about it." She frowned. "Is this just the beginning of realizing how much I don't know about my *own* husband?"

Claudia reached over and patted Karen's hand, saying softly, "Dear, you can think that you should already know this, and feel bad. Or you can get excited about what lies ahead. I recommend spending your energy thinking about how you will apply this information, instead of thinking about how you should have already."

Karen looked up at Claudia and smiled, her eyes clear now, and mischievous. She said, "You're pretty tricky, aren't you? You already made me promise that I wouldn't spend my time invalidating myself. How did you know this was going to happen?"

Claudia felt a new warmth for Karen. "Remember I told you that my mother and grandmother didn't start actively teaching me about men until I was sixteen? They did that on purpose. By then, I had already made mistakes with my brothers, my father, and a handsome boy I knew. Regret is a powerful teacher. To dwell there is not productive, but to visit can seal a lesson in a woman's heart and mind like nothing else."

Again, Claudia watched as Karen absorbed what she had said. Her admiration grew as she observed the young woman's ability to deal with many new ideas at one time.

Claudia asked, "Shall I continue or have you had enough for today?"

"You said that Knight was the second stage and that it begins at puberty, which I believe is around eleven or twelve years old. Since I teach second graders, who are only seven or eight, I would love to know about the stage before Knight."

Claudia was glad to see that Karen, all on her own, was already applying the information to men besides Mike. Another good sign.

"Great. Now that we have talked about Knights, we can talk about the preceding stage. We call these young men Pages. If you've watched any movies about Camelot, or read *The Once and Future King*, King Arthur first met Merlin when he was a Page. His ambition was to be a Knight. This is the easiest way to understand Pages. To apply a term often used today, you can think of them as 'Knight Wannabees.' Pages have adventures on a smaller scale and dream of owning a real horse. Today, you could translate that to a driver's license and a car."

Karen laughed, "You sure can. Most of the boys in my class can tell you exactly how many years and months until they turn sixteen. And most of them know the first car they want."

Claudia smiled and resumed, "That's great that you can see that. What I'm about to tell you, I'm sure you'll see in your students as well. Pages are very interesting and they're very interested in the world. They are also compelled to risk. They will drive their mothers crazy by climbing the tallest thing, lifting the heaviest thing, and endangering their lives in any other way that they can figure out. Boredom is intolerable to these little men."

Claudia paused. "I remember when my mother first told me about this. I was never bored and I couldn't understand why my little brother became bored often and why it seemed painful to him. My mother explained that girls and women are rarely bored because we pay attention to many things at one time. She told me that men only pay attention to one thing at a time. She said that boredom is when they can't find anything worth paying attention to."

"So the next time my little brother said he was bored, I asked him what that was like. He looked at me with such a pained expression and said, 'Oh, Sis, it's like dying real slow.'" Claudia chuckled. "I never made fun of him again. Instead, whenever he said he was bored, I helped him find something worth his attention. It wasn't all kindness—I knew from past experience that if I didn't help him find something good to pay attention to, he might find something himself that would annoy the heck out of me!"

Karen laughed. "I really shouldn't be laughing. My boys have told me that they were bored 100 times already this year. And I've always thought it was an indication of a lack of imagination. Oh dear, I guess I need to spice up my classroom. If Pages are Knight Wannabees, then they need fun and adventure too, right? If I put my mind to it, I could make their education a lot more challenging and a lot more interesting."

Claudia felt happy. To know that already her information might make those little men's lives better made her heart sing. "Something else you want to apply to the Pages in your classroom: Pages love to be your hero. If you can give them meaningful ways to help you, you'll see a real change in the way they regard you. Especially try it with the most difficult boys. Men of all ages become surly when they're not needed."

Claudia sat quietly while Karen's notes caught up with her. Mentally, she reviewed what she had set out to accomplish. There was just one piece left to give Karen today. When Karen stopped writing and looked up, Claudia asked, "What does Mike know about what you're doing today?"

Karen looked uncomfortable. "I only told him that I was having lunch with a new friend I met at the yoga center. Saturday is 'car day' for him, so it wasn't a problem. And since we haven't been spending much time together lately, I'm sure it wouldn't have been a problem anyhow. I'm not sure what to tell him about what we're doing here. Do you have any advice?"

"I'm glad you asked. As a matter of fact, I do have some recommendations. First, I recommend that you include Mike in what you're learning here. This information can help him understand himself as much as it will help you to understand him. Also, it could give the two of you something to talk about that isn't momentous or requiring a decision or commitment on his part."

Karen's large brown eyes grew rounder. "I never told you Mike was having trouble with decisions or commitments. Or did I?"

Claudia felt sympathy for Karen. She said gently, "Monday night at the coffee house you told me enough for me to see where Mike is in the Stages of Development. Consistent with that is a difficulty with commitments and decisions."

Karen responded quickly, "Can we talk about that stage today?"

Claudia sighed, "No, I'm sorry, not today. We have another significant stage to talk about that may take a couple of sessions, before we can get to where Mike is. Be patient; we will get there. And in between, I'll keep giving you information that will help you with Mike. For example, I recommend that you tell Mike about me and include what you promised me today. When you begin to talk about the information itself, when you tell him about Knights and Pages, it will work well if you tell him that you heard something interesting and would like his opinion about it. I know you saw things about him when he was in the Knight stage. It would be better to let him talk about it, before you tell him any of your observations. Okay?"

Claudia noticed Karen nodded without enthusiasm.

"One more thing," Claudia said, "When he's talking, do your best not to interrupt. Knowing how to listen to men is one of the *big* keys to the kingdom. Don't interject more questions or your thoughts when he's speaking. Notice every time you want to say something and hold your tongue—just keep listening. Even when he pauses or seems finished. Count to ten, if you have to, before saying anything. Do you think you can do that?"

Karen nodded her head again slowly and said, "I think I can. I will certainly try. Why is not interrupting important?"

"As I already mentioned, men think very differently than women. This affects the way they communicate. If you interrupt a man while he is speaking, it's like running a train off its track. He doesn't get back on track and keep talking. He will usually, with just a few interruptions, stop talking altogether. This is one of the reasons why women think men are shallow. We interrupt them before they can get to the best part of what they could have said."

Claudia could tell that all of the information she had given Karen today had worn Karen out. It was almost four o'clock. More tiring than the information was the shift in thinking it provoked. Claudia sensed both the past and the future had started to change for Karen today.

Claudia walked Karen to the door and there she saw further signs of Karen's disorientation. At the front step, she looked around like she couldn't remember where she had parked her car. Her heart swelling with compassion and appreciation for the younger woman's courage, Claudia impulsively hugged Karen and held her a little longer than was polite.

On the other hand, Claudia felt great. It was as if her knowledge had been weighing her down. In sharing it with someone, she felt lighter, younger, and suddenly satisfied. She was looking forward to telling Burt about their first session.

Mike realized he was prowling around the house. He had expected Karen to be back a couple of hours ago and wasn't sure what to do with himself. When Karen told him that she had a lunch date with a new friend from her yoga class, Mike was not alarmed. For many years, they had spent the first part of Saturday doing their own thing. Mike usually needed time alone and time with his cars to recover from the workweek. Karen usually needed time with other "grown-ups," either shopping or talking with her friends, after spending the week with second graders.

The day had begun like any other Saturday. Mike left about 8:00 A.M. to go toodling around the back roads in his little red Miata. The fresh air, the sunshine, and pushing the limit as he went up the winding curves of the Angeles Crest Highway, all came together to quiet his thoughts and bring him as close to peace as he was able to get these days.

By the time he returned, Karen had already left and he had the house to himself. He watched TV, surfing the various sports and automotive channels included in their cable package. By now, he'd also eaten and napped and was ready to spend time with his wife.

Where the hell is she? A luncheon can't take more than four hours, can it? He immediately realized that, with women, it easily could. A bunch of guys wouldn't spend much more than an hour at lunch, even spittin' and chewin' about their favorite topics. Remembering Karen was at lunch with another woman calmed him down a bit. Then he thought, but she said she was having lunch at a "friend's" house. Did she ever specify a woman?

These doubts were new for Mike. He and Karen had always had a satisfying, if not terribly exciting, sex life. But like other forms of communication, it also had broken down in the last eight months. He knew that the distance he kept from Karen and everyone else in his life had to have an effect. Admit it, he thought, you just don't want to do it that often.

Did Karen have needs he hadn't noticed? Damn! Just as his mind began generating pictures of imaginary couplings between his wife and other men, he heard the garage door open.

Mike quickly positioned himself on the couch with the remote control as if he had been sitting there for hours. He tried to appear calm as Karen entered the room. But immediately he noticed a difference in her, a lightness in her step, and as she turned toward him, he saw something in her face that he hadn't seen for a long time. She was kind of…happy. His heart jumped into his throat. He hoped she didn't notice the strangled "hi" that emerged. He thought, please God, don't let that be it.

As Karen drove home, she wished she didn't live close to Claudia. Of course, if they didn't live close, what were the chances they would have ended up in the same yoga class? Thinking she needed more time before she faced Mike, she pulled into the parking lot of her favorite coffee house and went in. She realized it was the same coffee house in which she had poured her heart out to Claudia five days before. Wow, she thought, if I had any idea who I was talking to, would I have told her as much? If I hadn't told her as much, would she have picked me? What exactly has she picked me for? Remembering that Claudia said she was only going to teach her what she thought she could use, Karen immediately wondered what she would be missing out on. Be content, she thought, I don't even know exactly what to do with what I've heard so far.

What *have* I heard so far? Karen's ordered mind demanded that she organize what she had been told today. Without noticing, she was automatically thinking of Claudia's information like a teacher designing a new curriculum. She sipped her cappuccino and made some notes on her pad.

When she looked at her watch, another forty-five minutes had passed. As she got in her car and headed for home, she thought, Time to face the music.

Face the music? Why would I think that? I've done nothing wrong. She thought of her promise to Claudia to be honest. She asked herself, have I been honest with Mike? Interesting that she would promise a woman she had just met something that she didn't provide her husband. But I don't lie to him, she thought. No, I just don't tell him things I think he won't like to hear. Instantly she recognized what Claudia had been talking about: she did treat Mike like an adversary. She didn't treat him with trust and respect, as much as she thought she trusted and respected him. Feeling full of promises today, she promised herself to try harder, to treat Mike like a partner. What is a partner? she wondered as she pulled into the garage.

When she entered the family room from the garage, she saw Mike sitting on the couch watching TV. She could tell by the tension in his shoulders that he was upset. She wanted to turn around and go out the way she had come in, but instead, her new promise fresh in her mind, she sat down across from him.

"Hi," he said. He sounded like he was choking on something. What can he be upset about? she wondered.

She started, "Are you busy? Are you hungry? I want to tell you about my afternoon."

Mike croaked out, "I'm not sure I want to know."

Karen was confused. "Why do you say that?"

"Well, things haven't exactly been great between us." He snarled, "It's almost five o'clock, you're a beautiful woman and you had lunch at a 'friend's' house. It doesn't take a genius to put it all together."

Karen was shocked and relieved. And flattered. *Beautiful?* Without meaning to, she laughed out loud. "I'm sorry. It's just that what you are talking about is the furthest thing from my mind. I spent the afternoon with a very wise woman who, as attractive as she may be, is just not my type!"

Karen could see Mike visibly relax. Was that a blush she saw? Poor thing. He thought I was with another man!

She wanted to touch him, to comfort him, but she was afraid of how he might react. She never knew what to expect from him these days. But she really wanted to tell him about Claudia and the Knights and Pages. She had an idea.

"Mike, how about we go out for a bite to eat? I'll tell you what we talked about today and see what you think about what Claudia said."

Mike got up from the couch and Karen took that as a "yes" to her idea. As he grabbed his keys to her car, he asked, "What was the subject?"

With everything about Mike uncertain, every sign of normalcy comforted Karen. For years they had taken her car instead of his truck when they were together. Lately, Mike had always insisted on driving his new Miata with the top down. Her hair blew all over the place. As she happily settled herself in her Honda sedan's passenger seat, Karen replied, "Men."

Mike snorted, "That's a simple subject. What did you talk about the rest of the time?"

"Really? Do you think men are simple? Because I thought I understood men. Lately, I just thought I didn't understand you. Now, after finding out that the women in Claudia's family have studied men for twenty-five generations, I'm thinking I don't even know how *much* I don't know!"

Mike seemed irritated. "Is this a woman thing? Are you sure you should tell me about it?"

Karen was glad for the opening. "Claudia specifically told me that I should tell you about her and tell you what I am learning. She said it would help you, too."

Karen saw Mike bristle and wanted to kick herself. He said harshly, "What makes her think I need help?"

Karen gently touched his arm. "Please don't be upset. You know how difficult things have been the last eight months or so. You don't seem like yourself. Please just listen to what I have to tell you. I think you'll find it interesting. Without my telling her, Claudia guessed that you're having trouble making decisions and commitments."

"What's wrong with that?" he demanded.

"Nothing," she persisted, digging the hole deeper. "That's what I'm trying to tell you. Apparently it has something to do with a stage you are in."

"What do you mean, a 'stage' I'm in? Like a child?"

Karen was relieved to see them pulling in to one of their favorite local restaurants. Mike had been trying a lot of new places lately. Again, it was comforting to see the old and familiar.

Trying to rescue the conversation, she turned to him and said, "No, according to Claudia, it's quite the *manly* thing to do." She raised her eyebrows suggestively as she said "manly." He couldn't help but chuckle and she breathed a little easier.

She got out and, speaking over the top of the car, said, "Let's wait until we get inside and order, then I'll tell you all about it."

After Mike had recovered from the shock of his own wild imaginings, he started to hear what Karen was saying. It sounded like this Claudia person had some interesting ideas. And Karen was animated. That by itself was worth it. Mike became more relaxed and was surprised to notice that he was actually enjoying himself. For Karen's sake, he had picked an old favorite of hers. He didn't much care for the place anymore, but he wanted her to be happy and she seemed to be. He wasn't sure if it was the restaurant or Claudia that had made her happy, but as long as it wasn't that other thing, it was fine by him.

After awhile, he said, "Let me see if I've got this right. Claudia is probably in her sixties. She is the last of twenty-five generations of man researchers and she has picked you to share her knowledge. Why did she pick you?"

He noticed Karen shift in her seat uncomfortably. She said, "Well, apparently something I told her made her think that I am not totally against you. Even though it's normal for women to treat men like enemies, apparently I don't always do that. She noticed ways that I'm sensitive to your needs and that I truly want to support you."

"It took a lot for you to say that, didn't it?" Mike asked.

Again, Karen shifted around. She looked down as she replied, "I promised Claudia that I would be honest with her. And I promised myself I would be honest with you. I am trying to treat you like my partner, even though no one has ever taught me how."

At that moment, she looked up at him. He could see the vulnerability in her eyes and he ached for her. He reached across the table and gently took her hand. "I've always thought of you as my partner. And I always thought you were doing the best you could."

"Well, I'm finding out I can do a lot better."

"Oh, Honey," he consoled her. "Don't be hard on yourself."

"Funny you should say that. Claudia made me promise something just like that."

"Really? What did she make you promise?"

Karen looked down again. He noticed her take a deep breath. Then, with obvious effort, she looked directly at him and said, "She made me promise not to purposefully use what I learn to hurt you and to forgive myself for not already knowing it. Something like that. I guess since I promised, I should find out exactly what it was."

"What an interesting promise. Did she ask you for anything else? Is she charging you?"

"No, she doesn't seem to want any money. She also asked that I tell only you what we talk about, and that we finish what we start." Karen added, "She thinks it will take about a month, meeting every week like we did today."

Mike frowned. "Will you be gone as long each time?"

"I don't think so. Today there was a lot of groundwork to lay. Kind of like the first day of school."

"Good. I may need my alone time, but I don't need as much as I got today." That was as close as he could come to admitting his fears.

He forced a small smile. "I missed you."

He could see that Karen liked hearing that. It made him wonder what else he hadn't been saying to her lately. *Man, I am really wrapped up in myself, aren't I? Look how pretty she is. When was the last time I noticed that?* Mike watched Karen as she toyed with her pasta, twirling it with her fork around and around. He loved her face. The smooth curve of her cheekbones. The way her nose made her look exotic. He was enchanted by her deep, golden brown eyes and thick lashes. He loved her full lips that were quick to smile. Or used to be, he corrected himself.

Brought back to the present, he said, "So, tell me about these stages. What stage am I in? The terrible forties?"

"I don't know yet what stage you're in. Claudia told me about the first two and she said she has another one to cover before we get to yours. How she already knows what stage you are in is beyond me. Sometimes I think she reads minds."

"What are the first two stages?" he asked.

"I'll tell you the same way she told me, starting with the second one. It really is easier to understand that way. For someone who has never shared her information, Claudia is a pretty methodical teacher."

Karen took a sip of her wine. "Anyway, the second stage goes from puberty—that happens around eleven-and-a-half, my child development books said—late into the twenties or even early thirties. They call them Knights. You know, the knights in shining armor, like Lancelot and the Round Table. She says men in this stage are all about fun and challenge and adventure. Seems they can't get enough of it."

Karen paused. "Do you want to tell me what you think, or should I keep going?"

"Keep going," Mike said. He liked to get all the information at once, think about it, and then draw his conclusions.

"Okay. The stage before Knights, they call Pages. Same era—you know, the little guys who followed the Knights around and idolized them. Claudia calls them 'little men' and says to think of them as Knight Wannabees. It was funny to hear an older woman use that term. Anyway, she says Pages need adventure, too, and drive their mothers crazy taking any risks they can find. That is sure true of my boys. Seems like half my job is keeping them safe and then trying to educate them."

Mike noticed Karen pause, like she thought she had said too much. Then she finished, "That's all I can remember without my notes. What do you think? Does the idea of stages hold water?"

Mike could tell by how high her voice went that the answer was important to her. Even if he hadn't seen some truth in what she had said, he might have fudged just to not rain on her parade. Karen this excited about something was worth preserving. But he was surprised. As Karen spoke of Knights, he could definitely see himself as a teenager, and even in his twenties. And while he couldn't remember much of himself as a Page, he could remember his younger twin brothers at that age. They drove his mother crazy. They lived in a two-story house and his brothers would jump from the highest stair they could. They narrowly made it to the bottom, and usually tumbled on the carpet. A few skinned knees and noses never stopped them from going higher and higher. When they got taller and could reach it, they slid down the banister in more and more dangerous positions, including upside down and backwards.

Mike said, "It looks like she's got something there. Remember all those jobs I had while you were finishing your degree?"

He paused, but Karen just nodded. "Well, after I learned how to do what they wanted from me, it got boring really fast. It just wasn't any fun going through the same thing over and over again. There wasn't any challenge in it."

He paused again, expecting her to comment. But she didn't say anything; she just looked interested. "That's why I loved the Peace Corps. There were always new challenges, either from the work or the conditions or the different cultures."

Karen still looked interested. And she still didn't say anything. "I've probably stuck with my business for as long as I have because no job is the same. Every time, there are new challenges, new problems to solve. It's been fun figuring out how to give each client what they want."

He thought about what he had just said. Only half-joking, he stated, "I thought you said the Knight stage goes until the early thirties. I'm forty-two and I might still need that challenge. Does that mean I'm developmentally handicapped?"

Karen shook her head. "I don't think so. One of things I forgot to tell you is that Claudia said men are always some part Knight, no matter how old they get. She said men always need challenge and adventure to some degree."

She paused and looked down. He could tell she was uncomfortable again. He waited and she continued, "I think I forgot to tell you because Claudia said it is really important for women to know how much adventure and challenge their men need. I was embarrassed that I never thought of that. I have no idea what you need or where you get it."

Mike felt sorry for Karen again. Boy, he thought, I hope every session with Claudia isn't as hard on her. But he noticed that it didn't seem to be a bad kind of hard. While Karen seemed ashamed about what she didn't already understand, she was still talking to him about it. This was the best conversation they had had in months.

On impulse, Mike got up from his seat and sat down on the other side of the booth next to Karen. He put his arm around her shoulder and squeezed. She leaned her head against him and he kissed her hair. Holding her, he said, "Honey, I think it's great what you learned today. And I'm glad you want to understand me. I think you were right. I think Claudia might help us both."

She turned her head and looked up at him. Her eyes were shiny, from happiness or sadness, he wasn't quite sure. She asked, "Will you tell me, please? How much adventure you need? How much challenge you need? And where you get it?" Her voice lowered. "Do you need challenge *from me*?"

It was easy to tell the last question was the most important to her. "Darlin'," he said in his favorite mock cowboy accent, "I get all the challenge I need when I walk out the door in the mornin'. What I need from you is soft arms to hold me and a smile to warm me."

He pulled her closer to him and spoke normally. "Seriously, I would have to think about it. I can tell you right now that you were a challenge when we first met. Smart and feisty. I loved that. But I don't think I want that now. I like us being comfortable with each other."

He noticed she was still listening. He continued, "I'd like us to have more fun together. But since I haven't been able to have fun by myself lately, I don't know how we would do that."

That felt too close for comfort. He changed directions. "I'm not sure how much challenge I need. Up until a few months ago, I would have said that I needed a lot. And I got a lot. Between my job and fixing my cars, I had plenty. But my job isn't what it used to be. I'm antsy. I get frustrated by the kind of problems I used to solve for fun."

He paused and said, half to himself, "Maybe I need a new kind of challenge."

Karen just kept looking up at him, obviously interested in what he might say next. But he didn't have anything else to say. Impulsively he leaned down and kissed her full on the mouth. Hmmm. *That* was fun. So he kept kissing her…and kissing her…and kissing her. Whoa, Cowboy, he thought, better get this filly on home.

Shortly after he saw Karen leave, Burt put away his tools, turned out the lights and left his workroom. He was hungry and curious. He found Claudia in the kitchen, where she immediately handed him a box of Cheese-Its. He leaned against the cupboards and munched away, watching her move deftly about the kitchen, putting dinner together. When he'd curbed his hunger, he set the table.

When they were settled at the dining room table, he said, "So, honey, how'd it go?"

He was rewarded with a big smile that crinkled her face all the way up to her lovely eyes. "That well, huh?"

As Claudia began to talk, Burt settled himself in to listen. Listening to Claudia was one of his favorite things to do. He loved everything about it. The way her voice rose and fell like a melody. The way her excitement lit up her face and, it seemed, the whole room. And the way her ideas had always surprised and intrigued him.

She said, "I think it went really well. Better, even, than I expected. Karen is a good student, which is rare for a teacher. She listens and asks good questions. I think this whole process is going to be really interesting. I am already anxious to find out what she does with what I told her today."

"What did you tell her today?"

"I told her about my family and what we have done for five hundred years. I didn't tell her about the Covenant, though. That's on my head, not hers. Then I began with the Stages of Development."

Burt cheerfully obliged by asking, "Tell me again, what are the Stages of Development?"

Claudia's eyes crinkled again with a smile. "It's the way men change as they get older. It happens in stages and it's predictable. They each last ten to fifteen years or more."

"What stage does that put me in, then? The sixth one?"

Claudia chuckled. "Actually, there are only four stages. The last one, the one we call King, usually lasts until the end of a man's life. But you are in a rare category, a *state* more than a stage. We call you an Elder."

"What's an elder? Is that just because I'm old?" he teased.

"No, Sweetie, it is not because you are old," Claudia smiled. "An Elder is a King who goes through a fairly quiet but dramatic transformation. In a way, it is like his life is over. But not in a negative way. His life is over in the sense that he has nothing else to prove; he has no agenda; he is beyond ambition. He spends his time focused on contributing to others and on enjoying and appreciating all the gifts in his life. This gives him a unique insight into people and into life itself. Elders are the wise men in our communities."

Burt was flattered, even as he recognized that what Claudia said was true. "It is an interesting way to live. I was used to striving for something. I always had something else to accomplish. Something I had to do or something I wanted to provide for you or the kids. Then, all of a sudden, it was gone. The ambition disappeared. I was done. I was content."

"I remember when it happened to you," she said. "It was about five years after you retired. You had been busy with all the projects you had planned and all the trips you wanted us to take. Remember? You had just finished carving the table and chairs for the garden, and they were magnificent. I wondered what you were going to build next and how you were going to top yourself. I expected it, because you had been working in such a flurry for such a long time. And then you just stopped. You became really calm. And you sat sit still for long periods of time."

She continued, "It was strange at first. I was used to your busyness, your appetites, your ambitions." She smiled, "But I got used to you again, after awhile. Now, I like how peaceful you are."

She added with a mischievous twinkle, "But I miss your opinions, because they sparked such interesting conversations."

Burt considered this. He hadn't thought about it before. It was true, though. He still had a lot of opinions about a lot of things. But he used to offer them to anyone he thought needed them. And then he stopped. Why was that, he wondered? Oh, I know, it's because it's a lot of responsibility telling people how to live their lives. I just didn't need the stress.

"Do you really miss my opinions?"

"Well," Claudia replied with a smile, "I've learned to ask for them when I want advice. But sometimes I need advice and don't know it. In the past, you always just provided it. It was hard to hear, but I would eventually come around and see that you had very valid points."

She continued, "I think it was harder for Myra, though. She always had a lot to prove to you. She hated getting her father's advice. She was afraid you gave it because you thought she couldn't figure it out on her own. I know that's not why you gave her unsolicited opinions. I know you hated to see her fail or be in pain. But she didn't understand that."

Burt sighed, "Yes, I can see I made many mistakes there. I just wanted to help her. Now, I don't offer advice because I've figured out that if people don't ask for it, it is unlikely they'll hear it, let alone follow it."

Claudia laughed. "Honey, that is actually great advice right there. I'm going to remember that with Karen and make sure she is asking for what I have to give."

Burt smiled, glad to have contributed to her project. "Is there anything else you said to Karen that you want to tell me about?"

"Actually, there were things that I didn't tell Karen, that maybe I should have. Since she was already taking herself to task over the mistakes she saw, I didn't want to point out any others. There are a lot of mistakes women make from not understanding the Stages of Development."

"Like what?"

"Well, for instance, we were talking about Pages. That's the first stage that goes from birth to puberty. Women, especially their mothers, don't understand these little guys and they expect things that are unreasonable."

"Like what?" he asked again.

"Well, like expecting them to be hygienic. They are going to get dirty and stay dirty and that's just the way of it. You can clean them up, but don't chastise them for getting dirty in the first place. Or, like expecting them to be modest about their accomplishments or their bodies. They brag and they flaunt. Or expecting them to understand why they shouldn't burp and break wind in public. They think it's fun and it's funny and there is no way they will ever understand why their mom thinks it isn't. She just seems uptight to them."

Burt was laughing. He could easily remember his own mother screaming at him and his brothers. Then he remembered Claudia with their son in the same situation. She had just pinned him with those eyes of hers and firmly said, "I understand your fun. And, *I need* you to *not* do that around *me*." Max was no fool—he caught on right away.

Burt was enjoying this. "Any other mistakes women make with Pages?"

Claudia replied, more serious, "The worst one is expecting these little men to be little women. We try to grind and groom and nag and beat the boy right out of them. We try to turn them into little girls. And we think that if we were better mothers, we could."

Burt nodded. "Did you just talk about Pages today?"

"No. We talked about Knights, too. That's the stage after Pages. It lasts from puberty to twenty-six or seven, or later, depending on a man's culture, personality and, even, birth order."

"What do you mean? How can it vary that much?"

"The Knight stage is all about fun and adventure and challenge. When a man gets serious about building something—that's what the stage after Knight is all about—depends on many things. First-born males tend to be ready for responsibility sooner. And some cultures are more serious and ambitious than others. Then, of course, some individuals are just more serious than others."

"That sounds interesting," Burt said. "I remember when fun and adventure were everything. But I was the oldest, and I was expected to do certain things. In a way, I think I was glad to join the Navy at the beginning of the War to avoid all that responsibility. The Navy was a way I could go off on an adventure and still be well thought of."

Claudia smiled, remembering. "And you were so handsome in your uniform. But I was heartbroken when you volunteered. I thought you wanted to get away from me. Then my mother explained Knights to me. That saved me from making a lot of other mistakes."

"What kinds of mistakes do women make with Knights?" Burt asked.

He watched while Claudia thought for a moment. He liked the way she pursed her lips while she was thinking. He thought it was cute.

She said, "Women make a lot of mistakes at this stage, and mostly for the same reason: We take everything personally. This is the stage when women are first getting involved with men romantically. And there is too much we don't understand. We think that if you really loved us, you wouldn't want to spend time with your friends and you wouldn't go off and do things that seem crazy or silly to women. We think that if we were prettier, or gave you the sex you wanted, that we could keep you with us."

Burt shook his head sadly.

Claudia kept going, "One that makes me sad is that we panic every time you notice another woman. We are scared and hurt and bury it under anger. Women don't know how vulnerable men are to women's looks. A woman thinks that the man purposely turned his head to look at the other woman. She thinks if he really loved her or cared about her, he wouldn't look. She doesn't know that the other woman literally turned his head and there wasn't a darn thing he could do to prevent it. The best he can do is get whiplash from turning it back fast enough, trying not to get caught."

Burt smiled, remembering. "I used to wonder about that. My friends were always in trouble for looking. Their girlfriends or wives just took them apart. But you never did. Whenever I found myself looking, when I turned back to you, you just smiled and kept talking like nothing happened."

Claudia nodded. "That's just it. Nothing had happened. Would I have been mad if you had tripped? Like that was something against me? That's all it was. She tripped you."

She continued, "Now I know that there are men who look on purpose, for a long time. They usually do that to put the woman they're with in her place. But he only feels the need to do that if she has been diminishing him in some way, or making him feel out of control, or giving him the impression that she thinks he's not good enough for her."

Burt marveled at Claudia's wisdom. He wished more women knew what she knew. What a lot of pain and suffering it would prevent, he thought.

"Are there any other mistakes women make with Knights?" he asked.

"Well, there is another that is related to what we just talked about. Women understand that men are 'visual,' but when they say it, it's almost always nasty—like men shouldn't be that way. But what women don't understand is how visual men are—how acute that sense is, and how many things they can tell about a woman just by looking at her."

"Really? Like what?" He was wondering if he knew himself.

Claudia smiled. "Just to name a few: A man can tell by the way she carries and moves her body if she is aggressive or receptive, impatient or used to being in control. He can tell if she is self-confident, or unsure of herself, putting on airs, or relaxed and comfortable.

"When a man looks at a woman's face, he can see much more than the shape and organization of her facial features. Women who are bitter have what men call 'a pinched look.' Resentment develops 'edges' in a woman's face and makes her look 'sharp.' She looks intimidating; no matter how lovely her features might be otherwise. Our faces can have an overall look of being clouded or muddled when we are upset or angry. Men tend to keep their distance when we look like this. On the other hand, when a woman is happy, her face gives off a light or glow that draws people to her. Being at peace—with herself or the world—is reflected in a 'softness' of the cheeks, jaw, mouth and eye area that makes a woman look approachable."

She laughed. "Okay, that wasn't just a few. But that's just her body and her face. Her eyes are the most revealing."

Burt smiled, letting her lead him along. "Really?"

She dimpled. "They show everything from sadness to joy, skepticism to acceptance. When we are critical or judgmental, our eyes show it—the pupils contract and our eyes look 'hard.' When we are interested in something or someone, our eyes shine or sparkle. Passion makes our eyes 'light up.' Most men have said that the most attractive feature in any woman is her eyes."

"Remember Pete at the Chamber of Commerce?" she asked.

Burt nodded.

"He told me, 'The most extraordinary thing is to look into a woman's eyes and see that she accepts you.' Another man, at the Veteran's Administration, in his late forties, said, 'When a woman looks at you and her eyes are sparkling, it's like she gives you a small piece of her spirit.'"

Burt smiled, aware that that was happening to him right now.

Later, lying in bed with Claudia curled against him, he thought, for the thousandth time, how blessed he was. His life was full of good things and good people. In perfect contentment, he fell asleep.

Karen lay curled against Mike, listening to him snore softly. Her hand lay on his chest, buried in curly brown hair. She was almost giddy with excitement. Oh my, she thought, all I did was listen! Who would have thought? Claudia would have thought, she told herself. Oh, I don't know about that, she mentally argued back, reliving the lovemaking that had recently concluded. I don't think she could have anticipated that! Well, she does call what she knows the *"keys to the kingdom"*…

Whether or not Claudia knew the power of what she had told Karen that day, Karen was more grateful, already, than she could have imagined. That night, instead of staying as far over on her own side of the bed as possible, she fell asleep on Mike's. As she drifted off, she thought, he said I am beautiful…

In place of the tears that she had become used to, a smile accompanied her to sleep.

The Men Who Would Be Kings

Brrrrriiiiiinnnnnnnngggggg! The final bell sounded and most of the kids jumped up from their seats and headed for the door in a rush. Casey was hanging back a bit and Karen smiled to herself. Looking around, she spotted something for him to do.

"Casey?" He paused and turned toward her. "Do you have to go home right away? I have some stuff I could sure use your help with."

She noticed Casey's small shoulders straighten a bit. He came back to her desk. "Watcha doin'?" he asked.

"Well," she said. "I need to take down all the Columbus pictures and put up the Thanksgiving feasts you guys made this week. I was hoping you would help me since I'll bet you're really good at hanging stuff up with tacks."

Casey smiled shyly. "Sure, Mrs. Trevino, if you say so."

As Karen worked with Casey, she marveled that this was the same boy who had disrupted her class since September. His normally sullen expression was gone and he was actually chatting with her as they worked. He *was* good at hanging things. And the more she noticed, the more he tried to do it well.

"You're doing a good job of getting the tacks right in the corner, Casey. You are precise. I like that quality in a man."

She noticed that Casey blushed but didn't protest. Did he just get bigger? She wondered. Seems like his chest kind of puffed up.

When they were finished, Karen thanked him. "I really like doing this stuff with you. You're a big help and you make it more fun, too." He rewarded her with a rare grin.

As Casey waved good-bye, Karen thought again about the change in him this week. On Monday, he had been his usual surly, sullen, unco-operative self. She had gotten used to it and thought she understood the cause. With two parents totally involved in their careers, Casey didn't get much attention at home. But his manner didn't invite her positive atten-tion. She usually wanted to avoid him or discipline him.

On Tuesday, Karen remembered what Claudia had told her about Pages. While it seemed impossible that Casey would ever want to help her, she thought she would give it a try. Remembering that he walked home, probably to an empty house, she had an idea. That day, as the other kids were leaving, she asked Casey to stay behind. He had stood at her desk, his small arms crossed across his chest with his hands tucked in his armpits, obviously waiting for the lecture or consequence he expected.

Instead Karen had said, "I'm thinking that you are probably the strongest boy in the class. Would you help me carry some boxes to the storage room?"

Casey had shrugged his shoulders but he immediately picked up a box. He followed her slowly down to the crowded storage room and set the box down near the door.

"That's great, Casey. Could you bring another one while I make some room for them?"

Again Casey shrugged but headed back to the classroom. Well, he hasn't bolted yet, she had thought. Karen rearranged some boxes to make room for hers. Shortly, Casey returned, this time carrying two boxes, one stacked on top of the other. He could barely see around the sides.

"Wow," she said. "You really *are* strong!"

Without her asking, he set down the two boxes and returned to the classroom for the lightest box. She noticed that he made a show of carrying it with only one hand, although it balanced precariously. Karen smiled, showing how impressed she was.

"I sure asked the right guy for help, didn't I?"

Casey shrugged again, but this time he spoke. "I guess so."

That was Tuesday. A similar thing happened on Wednesday, when he helped her make a bunch of copies in the office. She noticed how carefully he stacked the papers and commented on it. It was Thursday when she first noticed him hanging back as the others left. It was as if he hoped she would ask him for help. She asked him to put the next day's assignment on the board. She commented that board writing was difficult but he did it neatly.

By Friday, his classroom behavior had changed as well. He was paying attention instead of drawing or daydreaming or distracting the kids around him. He answered her questions now instead of just shrugging. She thought he seemed happier. Could all that have come out of her asking him for help? She would have to ask Claudia.

Karen was looking forward to seeing Claudia tomorrow for their second session about men. They had stopped for tea after yoga on Wednesday night and Karen had told her most of what had happened with Mike over the weekend. It was the best time she and Mike had had together since spring. Remembering Saturday night with a smile, she thought, being honest with Claudia doesn't mean I have to tell every detail, does it?

The next day, Claudia was pleasantly surprised that Karen had insisted on bringing lunch. Karen treated her to some salads from the local health food store and deli. She presented them to Claudia, saying, "The special oil they use in these salads is supposed to be good for your joints." Claudia thought it was neat that Karen wanted to give something back.

After lunch, they set their tea on the table outside and Claudia gave Karen a tour of her garden. She tried to make it short, but her enthusiasm took over and she found herself going on and on about her shrubs, vines, and flowers, their histories, and why she planted them where she did. Karen commented, "You are passionate about gardening, aren't you?"

Claudia laughed. "Yes, I am passionate about my garden. I love the dirt and the growing and the beauty that can happen. As you can tell, I can get to talking about it." She paused. "But I am even more passionate about women having something they are passionate about."

"What do you mean?" Karen asked.

Claudia was glad she asked. This was important to plant in Karen's mind before they got too far down the path they were on. She led Karen over to the table Burt had carved for her and settled in before answering.

She said, "What is normal for women instinctively is to focus on pleasing their men, and to avoid displeasing them. We naturally change and mold and even contort ourselves to be what we think they want. Since we do this automatically, we can lose ourselves without noticing. We just wake up feeling empty one day."

She could tell by Karen's expression that she had struck a cord. She continued, "It is very important for a woman to keep something in her life that has nothing to do with her husband or boyfriend. Something that expresses who she is as an individual. Something she is passionate about. This will help her to not lose herself in the relationship or in her family."

Claudia paused to let this sink in. She could see Karen's thought processes play across her face as she absorbed what Claudia had told her. She waited for Karen's features to clear, meaning she had finished ingesting the information and was ready for more.

Claudia then said, "As women, one of our strengths is our ability to adapt. It is a critical ability. I don't think humans would have survived without women being this way. But the other side of that ability is a weak sense of ourselves. At least compared to men."

Karen seemed surprised. "Men have a stronger sense of themselves? Really?"

Claudia nodded. "Yes, it is one of their many unique qualities."

Karen asked, "What are the others?"

Claudia smiled and patted Karen's hand. "Not today, dear. Today we're going to talk about the third stage in the Stages of Development. It has everything to do with this sense of self men have."

Karen pulled out her pad and pen. "Okay, I'm ready," she said.

Claudia began, "One day in their late twenties or early thirties, a Knight comes home from an adventure and notices he doesn't have much to show for himself. Suddenly, living for the present isn't enough. But when he looks to the future, it can be bleak. He sees that he has no castle, no queen, and no heirs. This is when he begins the stage we call 'Prince.'

She paused for a sip of tea. It had grown cold during the tour of her large garden. "The easiest way to understand a Prince is by recognizing what he is not. What do you think a Prince is not, Karen?"

Karen replied, excitedly, "He's not a king!"

"Exactly," Claudia said. "A Prince is not a King. And very quickly he becomes completely, painfully aware of that. He looks around and recognizes the men who are Kings. He can tell the difference between them and himself. They have something, and more importantly, they *are* something."

She continued, "So this phase is all about *becoming a king*. It is all about defining and creating his own kingdom, and in the process, defining and creating his own *self*."

Claudia noticed Karen rub her arms as if she felt a sudden chill. "Yes?" Claudia inquired.

Karen replied, "It seems exciting. How does he go about it?"

"Well," Claudia responded, "It happens in three different phases, all within this one stage called Prince."

She explained, glad to have such a curious listener, "The first phase we call Early Prince. During this phase a man has to figure out where to build his kingdom. In other words, what he wants to be King of. This is where that sense of self comes in again, because he has to find a career or line of work that *fits*. He may know instantly or he may approach many, many different things until he finds the work that feels right, that fits him. A man can be an Early Prince for a few minutes, or for many years. It will last as long as it takes for him to find his place."

Claudia paused to let Karen respond. She said, "I think Mike figured it out quickly. When we came back from Africa, he started his construction business by remodeling houses. He was off and running. I don't think he ever looked back. That is, until recently."

Claudia let the last remark go for now. She replied, "It sounds like his work in Africa helped him figure out what he wanted to do."

"I think so," Karen said. "He took part in a lot of different kinds of building projects—dams, sewage systems, schools. He loved helping the villagers build their own homes the most. He found some neat ways to use indigenous materials and get a lot out of a small space."

Claudia smiled and resumed, "After a man settles on his career, he enters the phase we call Middle Prince. This phase lasts between ten and twelve or thirteen years. He is intense about working and building his career. He is intense about establishing himself in whatever area he has chosen. He feels an urgency about it. A Prince is driven to accomplish and progress, and gets upset about any setbacks. He also has little time, energy, or attention for anything outside of what he is building. This can have a big effect on men's relationships."

Karen interrupted, "Does that mean they don't care about relationships? They're not interested in marriage?"

"Not necessarily," Claudia said. "It all depends on how they define their kingdom. There seem to be two main camps: the men who think having a partner to build with is essential; and the men who think that first you build the castle, then you find your queen."

She continued, "The first group is likely to get married not long after they figure out what hill they are going to conquer. They change from dating exciting, fun, and adventurous young women, to searching for their partner. That is the word they use the most: Partner. They are looking for someone they can trust and someone who is going in the same direction. They are looking for the person that will help them to succeed in building their kingdom."

Claudia saw a flicker of pain cross Karen's features. "What is it?" she asked.

Karen looked up, her golden brown eyes clouded. "Mike said that he always thought of me as his partner. But I'm not sure how good a partner I've been. How can you tell if you are a good partner?"

"Being a good partner to a Prince can be difficult," said Claudia. "Mostly, it means giving him what he needs, or helping him to find it."

"What do Princes need?" Karen asked.

"A Middle Prince needs many things. He needs his woman to be happy with what he is able to provide now. And not just the material things he provides. He needs the limited amount of time and energy and attention he can pay to be enough. He is painfully aware of being insufficient. He needs to feel good enough for her; he needs to feel successful with her. He also needs her to believe in him and encourage him. His wife or girlfriend believing in him can make all the difference. And he needs to hear it, often. He needs her praise and admiration."

Claudia chuckled, remembering, "He also needs mundane things. His attention is focused on what he is building and he is easily derailed by not having the simplest necessities. Things like socks, new underwear, clean clothes, and lunch money."

Karen seemed upset. Claudia heard resentment when she said, "I know I provided all those things for Mike. But it seemed like he never noticed. He certainly never *thanked* me."

Claudia felt sympathetic. "I'll tell you a secret, Karen. Men almost never thank you for giving them what they need. They just grab it and go back to doing what they were doing. It is part of the way they think, part of how focused they are. It is not meant to be unappreciative or a slight in any way."

She could tell Karen wasn't quite ready to accept that.

"What else about Middle Princes?" Karen asked.

"Well, let's see." Claudia thought for a moment, wondering how much she should say. She decided to try something.

"I'll tell you some mistakes women make with Middle Princes if you remember your promise to forgive yourself."

"Okay, I forgive myself in advance," Karen said emphatically, and leaned forward with her elbow on the table.

Claudia knew that in this position, Karen would feel less vulnerable, which was probably a good thing right now.

She began, "Alright, here you have it. A mistake almost every woman makes is expecting a Middle Prince to pay attention to everything happening in *her* life. She wants him to remember every event, important meeting, holiday and her personal preferences. With what he is focused on, he just cannot do it. And having birthdays or holidays be tests for him will just make them both miserable."

Claudia leaned forward, "Do you use a computer?"

Karen was surprised, "Yes, of course I do. Do you?"

"Burt bought one a few years ago to keep in touch with our grand-children in Oregon, our son's two boys. Burt got interested in computers and learned all about them, and of course, I've heard a great deal about them. One of the things Burt taught me about computers applies to Middle Princes."

"Really? No kidding."

"Absolutely. You know that thing they call RAM on a computer?"

Karen nodded.

"Well, think of RAM as how much you can have open on your computer screen at one time. Almost all the RAM a Middle Prince has is used up by what he is building. He can't also keep his wife or girl-friend's life on his screen at the same time."

Karen laughed at the image. "This certainly explains a lot of the fights Mike and I had. I definitely expected him to remember what was happening in my life. And I tested him, every birthday. He usually forgot it. What *should* I have done?"

"A woman needs to provide the information a man needs when he can act on it," Claudia replied. "This is one of the keys to the kingdom: providing men with useful information at the right time. With a Prince, you have to be a little tricky. Do you know those little annoying pop-up thingamajiggers that come on your screen when you're on the Internet?"

Karen nodded. "Well," Claudia said, "a woman with a Middle Prince has to be a pop-up on his screen from time to time. And it is most effective to be a happy pop-up."

Karen's head tilted to the side. "Can you give an example?"

Claudia thought a moment, chuckling at the memories. "Let's take your birthday. About a week ahead of time, you would say, 'Gee, I'm so…'"

She stopped. "No, I guess you wouldn't say 'Gee' would you? Okay, you would say, 'Wow, I'm so happy it's my birthday next Tuesday.' A few days later, you would tell him what you wanted to do for your birthday and make sure to ask if he can. Then, the day before your birthday, you would say, 'I can't believe it, when I wake up, I'll be thirty-nine!' In the morning you could say, 'Hey handsome, kiss the birthday girl!' You see what I mean about a happy pop-up?"

Karen barely nodded. "Sounds kind of silly. Does it work?"

Claudia nodded. "Yes, it really works. And not doing it can be disastrous. Every year for my birthday, while Burt was a Middle Prince, I was tempted to see if he would remember. Even with what I know, I'm still a woman, you see. We always want to know they're thinking about us. The year I didn't provide the pop-up, he completely forgot and was mortified. It was as if someone had let all the air out of his balloon. I felt terrible. I had set him up to fail."

Karen looked stricken. She agreed, sadly, "Yep, I've done that plenty of times."

Claudia felt compassion for Karen. This was a hard and important lesson to begin learning. She decided to retreat for now. She said, "How about I tell you some of the mistakes women make with Middle Princes—that I am guessing you *didn't* make?"

Karen said with a rueful smile, "That would be a relief."

Claudia said, "I'll tell you about women dating Middle Princes. I know you didn't do any of this since you married Mike when he was a Knight. Most of this happens because women are used to thinking of men as adversaries, not partners. This makes us think in manipulative terms instead of doing something that would empower a man.

"For a long time women have been taught a strategy of turning a man down for a weekend date if he doesn't call by Wednesday. I think this is supposed to make him think you are in high demand and work harder. With Middle Princes, though, it will completely backfire. On Wednesday, he is virtually under water with whatever he is building. He is not thinking about the weekend. It's not on the screen yet. On Friday night or Saturday morning—or Saturday night for the working-six-days-a-week Prince—he will change his focus from work to recreation. Now he is looking to renew himself. A great way for a man to do that is to spend some quality time with a woman. That is when he will think to call someone special and ask her out. If she is practicing the 'call by Wednesday' strategy, they'll never get together."

Karen said, "Wow, I've got friends who use that strategy. What a shame they don't know this. What *should* they do?"

"Well, if they are dating Middle Princes, forget that policy."

"So they should just wait around until he calls on the weekend? It would drive me crazy not knowing my weekend plans ahead of time."

"If they have been dating for awhile, more of a regular thing, *she* could certainly call *him* up ahead of time. She could call him on Wednesday and say something like, 'I'm figuring out my plans for this weekend. It would make me happy to spend time with you. Should I save Saturday night for us to do something together?' If she calls him at work, she should expect a response like, 'Sure.' And that's it. When the weekend comes around, then they can figure out what they are going to do."

Claudia continued, "Another mistake women make is pressuring Middle Princes into relationships. If he is the type that thinks that first you build the castle and then you move the queen in, he won't be ready to have a relationship. He may ask a woman out every week, but when she presses him to be her boyfriend, he'll say something like, 'I don't have time for a relationship.' The woman will try to convince him that it won't be more time than they spend now, but he knows better. For men, dating is something they do one date at a time. No strings. They know a relationship carries responsibilities in between dates."

Claudia could see it was working. Karen sat back in her chair, her arms at her sides. By talking about things that had nothing to do with her, Karen was starting to relax.

Claudia decided to go on. "After ten or twelve years, the Prince enters a new phase."

Karen interrupted, "Ten or twelve *years?*"

Claudia nodded. "Yes, ten or twelve years. Maybe longer."

Karen shook her head in disbelief.

Claudia continued, "We call this phase Late Prince. These men have many accomplishments under their belts. They have become more confident. You can see it in the way they walk and carry their heads. They can see the end coming and feel like they can ease up. They have more time and attention for other things now."

Karen seemed excited. As if she were bursting, she said, "That's where Mike was a year ago, I'm sure of it! Wow, it was great. He had spent all those years working such long hours. I got more involved in school so I wouldn't be home alone. Suddenly, *he* was asking to spend time with *me*, instead of the other way around. I backed out of some school committees to be with him. It was so much fun. I wanted it to last forever."

Claudia smiled in sympathy. "Alas, my dear, it can't. The period of being a Late Prince is a short one. I think it is a brief respite before the hardest part of all."

Karen asked, "What's that?"

Claudia shook her head. "Not today, dear. I know you are anxious to hear about where Mike is now. But I have filled your head enough. It will be much better for you to let this all sink in first."

Karen seemed anguished. "But what will I do until next week?"

"Oh, there is plenty to do. Talk to Mike about what you learned today. Tell him all about Princes. And then listen and listen and listen some more. This is a chance for the two of you to have closure, as they say, on an important part of both your lives. I recommend you think about the things you want to be appreciated for, and the things you want to apologize for. And then tell Mike. If he wants, Mike might do the same."

She continued, "From what you told me the other night, it sounds like you are doing a good job of practicing listening without inter-rupting. Keep working on that; it is the secret. Remember—keys to the kingdom. Men have a strong sense of themselves, but they only reveal who they are in special circumstances. By practicing listening in a way that works for Mike as a man, you'll be preparing for where he is now in the best way possible."

Seeing the pain and doubt in Karen's face, Claudia reached across the table and grasped Karen's hand. "Trust me," she said, holding Karen's gaze.

Karen nodded, quickly squeezed her hand, and got up. She asked, "Can we plan on coffee or tea after yoga on Wednesday night? It helps me to check in with you mid-week."

"Certainly, dear. I would love to," Claudia said.

Claudia walked her to the door and noticed a disorientation similar to last week. Karen stood on the stoop for a long moment, looking this way and that for her car. Finally, she set off with uncertain steps. Claudia came out on the porch and sat down in a wicker chair, watching Karen walk to her car. She stretched out her legs and closed her eyes, waiting for the sound of Karen's car starting.

Mid-morning on Saturday, Mike walked through his latest project, examining the finish work of the walls, custom cabinetry and elaborate molding. This tour was planned for yesterday, but another project had held him up. He needed to get this done today so the men could complete their work, starting early Monday morning. He would miss his morning drive, but since Karen was seeing the yoga woman again, he could go this afternoon.

To any observer, he would appear the same as he had for over a decade: methodically examining each detail and either checking the item off his list or making a note to change or fix something. He slowly worked his way through each room of the house.

To himself, though, nothing was the same. For years, as he completed a tour, he would marvel at the workmanship of his men and subcontractors, admiring his solutions to many design and implementation problems, and basically congratulating himself for another job practically finished and well done.

Today, as he proceeded from room to room in this 4,500 square foot, Westside home, he kept wondering how many of these rooms would ever get any real use. While individually he appreciated the accomplishment of the library, gaming room, mini-theatre, family room, formal dining room, living room, master suite, and bedroom/bathroom combinations for each of the teenage children, he couldn't help but think that altogether it was a waste of space and natural resources. If I had monitors in these rooms, he thought, tracking the time people spent in them each day, what would it show a year from now? How many would primarily log time being dusted by the maid?

Why am I thinking about this? *Oh, hell.* This is another one of those damn questions that come out of nowhere and plague me! I never thought about this *before*. I didn't *care* what my customers did with their homes. I cared if they were satisfied, if they paid me on time, if they referred me to their affluent friends. And that was enough.

But it wasn't enough anymore. It just didn't feel right to create these attractive rooms with no real purpose. They looked beautiful; they would certainly impress people, but they had no life in them and probably never would.

He wondered which room would become the hub of this family. Or would the abundance and variety of rooms keep them separate? God knows it is hard enough to keep teenagers and their parents interacting without providing all these ways to stay apart.

Unbidden, he remembered the dirt-floored homes he had built in Zimbabwe. To these people, they would have been scarcely one-room hovels. But to the local villagers, their new homes were beautiful, special places to laugh and eat and live together. Now, *there* was a worthy purpose!

And life! Those homes were full of life. Teaming with activity and noise. Not like this cavernous place would probably end up to be, no matter how dressed up it was.

Mike shook his head, trying to clear his thoughts. This wasn't getting him anywhere!

Finally finished with his tour and checklist, Mike went outside to eat his lunch before he took off. As he sat alone under a tree chomping on a sandwich, his thoughts turned to Karen. He felt—what was it? Oh! *Happy*. He felt happy. It had been so long, he barely recognized it.

Mentally, he played back last weekend. He skipped the angst he had felt waiting for Karen on Saturday. That was not worth revisiting. As he remembered, dinner with Karen took on the quality of a "date," like the kind they had had early in their relationship. Where the conversation was interesting and the conclusion was perfect. Imagine, married nearly twenty years, and they had a *date*. He felt giddy remembering it.

And I got laid! He chuckled to himself. When was the last time I thought in *those* terms, let alone thought that was some great accomplishment?

Things with Karen had been strained for such a long time, it *was* an accomplishment. Not because she hadn't been willing. Oh, no. Because *he* hadn't wanted to. Not for a while. And when he did, it was more from pressure building, not desire. It made the sex pretty perfunctory.

Tell the truth, lover boy, he said to himself. Very perfunctory. Just the basics.

Where did all that desire come from Saturday night? He wondered, feeling like a young stud again. The way she had looked at him, the way she had listened to him—it made his blood heat up. Fascinating. And the result. Wow. It had been a long, long time since they'd had "a session." A long time since he had touched her that much, feeling the exquisite softness of her caramel skin. Being touched by her small, feminine hands. Being held. Making love to her that way thoroughly changed his life—even a week later.

The rest of the weekend had been different, too. Karen was different. Calmer, quieter, listening a lot. And when she did talk, she was excited, not complaining, not nagging for a decision or commitment about something.

Could her time with—what's her name? Oh, yea, Claudia. Could her time with Claudia have anything to do with it? Hmmm. Wonder what she'll be like after today?

Karen sat in her car without turning the key. Tears slowly streamed down her face. Not because of the mistakes she had made with Mike. It was much worse than that.

She hadn't realized when she had committed to learning about men from Claudia, that she would be learning as much about women, and especially, about herself. *I guess it makes sense that you can't have* one without the other, she thought. But the more she learned, the more she lost. And what she was losing, she had never known she valued so highly.

She was losing the ability to blame Mike and his business for her life.

Thinking that any day he would start working less, start spending more time at home, and suddenly want to have children, she had put her life on hold. She had spent twelve years waiting, *one day at a time*. Not that Mike had asked her to. In fact, the opposite: he had encouraged her to pursue her interests, to get involved in things she liked.

Did he even know I was waiting for him? I don't think so. From what Claudia said, I think he was just being a Prince, doing what a Prince is compelled to do. No wonder my resentment was such a surprise.

I wonder if all women do this. It doesn't seem like it. I know lots of women with careers they pursue—almost like they were Princes themselves. But I don't want that, either. Most of them are alone. Or in relationships that seem distant. Is there something in the middle? Can I have a partnership *and* a life of my own?

Hmmm. Maybe they're connected. To have a partnership between two people probably takes two *whole* people. I've been half a person, waiting for the other half to come home. *Oops*. And I thought I was independent!

So, how do I become a whole person? Claudia said women adapt to men and contort themselves. I've certainly done that. Why did she say we do that? Oh, yea, to please men. If I *weren't* pleasing Mike—or waiting for Mike—what *would* I be doing?

Karen was surprised by the things that immediately popped into her head, as though a list had been just waiting for her to ask. Riding horses. Learning Spanish. Making babies.

At the last one, fresh tears started down her face. She could ride horses on her own. She could learn Spanish on her own. Babies? Every time Karen had brought up starting a family, Mike had said, "Not yet. I'm not ready yet." Damn it, he had been saying that for fifteen years!

A hundred times, Karen had thought about getting pregnant "accidentally." But she couldn't do it. She wanted the father of her children to be as excited about them as she was. So she'd waited. And poured herself into her students. Surely, they had benefited by being her only children. But Karen knew, at thirty-nine, that time was running out for her biologically.

Maybe I should bring it up again. No, wait. Talk to Claudia first. She had talked about Knights and children, and about Princes and relationships, but she hadn't said anything about Princes and children. Could Mike's thing about children have something to do with being a Prince? But lots of men in their thirties have children. Hmmm. Ask Claudia. She almost went back to the house to ask her now. That would be rude, she thought. She's probably busy with dinner or something.

As Karen started her car and put it in gear, she wondered if "Ask Claudia" was going to become her new mantra.

As Karen drove off, Claudia entered the house and went to the kitchen. She could see the light on in Burt's shop. Wondering what he was working on these days, she started preparing dinner. Knowing how much he loved surprising her, she would continue to pretend she hadn't noticed how much time he was spending in his shop. She would start asking about it when he was bursting to tell her.

As she chopped vegetables, she thought about her afternoon with Karen. With each session, her respect for her student grew. Her concern also grew. She was in what Burt would have called "uncharted waters." She knew she was giving Karen a lot of potent information in one session and that there was danger in it. But her own sense of urgency propelled her. And each session, Karen impressed her with her ability to absorb it all, with little resistance—even when Claudia knowingly touched tender places in Karen's life or identity.

Claudia was glad they had already planned to meet Wednesday night. A mid-session check-in with her student was a good idea. With the kinds of seeds—and bombs—she was planting in Karen's thinking, a lot could happen in four or five days.

Burt put his tools away, took one last admiring look at the bench-in-progress and shut off the light. As he walked from his shop to the house, he whistled *I'm Popeye the Sailor Man*.

He smelled dinner as he entered the house and smiled. Although they often enjoyed cooking together, somehow Claudia always knew when to start without him. Since he heard plates being set, he headed straight for the washroom to clean up.

Seated across from Claudia, in front of a steaming plate of food, Burt observed his wife eating with something that approached gusto. It warmed his heart to see her diving into her dinner the way she was diving into teaching Karen. This was all good. Very good.

"How did it go today, sweetheart?" he asked and took a bite.

Claudia nodded, smiled at him and kept chewing. She seemed satisfied.

"Want to tell me about it? What did you talk about?"

Burt waited while Claudia finished chewing, wiped her mouth with her napkin, and took a sip of her water. She eventually said, "We're talking about Princes."

"Really? The kind that come from frogs?" he teased.

Claudia chuckled. "That's a good one, honey. Especially since many women think men *are* frogs and are trying to kiss them into being Princes. If they only knew it works the opposite much more often."

Once again Claudia surprised him. "What do you mean *the opposite*?" he asked.

"Well," she said, "I believe men are naturally Prince-like—heroic, honorable, loyal, generous. Women manage to turn them into frogs."

"How do they do that?"

"Oh, you would know if you thought about it. Women do things that bring the worst out in men and then blame them for it. They attack men—with their words and voices as weapons, mostly—and incite the most primitive, instinctive, defensive reactions."

He was intrigued. "Is that what you talked to Karen about today? Sounds interesting."

"Actually, no. I'm not sure if I'll ever talk to Karen about that. It's a tough subject. I think I will just make her aware of the most common ways women do it, but one thing at a time, instead of the whole lot. Today we talked about Princes. Not the frog cousins, but the third stage of development. It was a great topic because the stage is recent for Karen and Mike."

"Will it help her with the problems she is having now?"

Claudia nodded. "I'm sure of it. Even though it's not the stage he is in now." She paused. "Actually Mike isn't in a *stage* right now. He's in a *transition*. Very uncomfortable." Burt's curiosity was further piqued as she shook her head in what he thought was pity.

She continued, "It should help them because Karen has a lot of misunderstandings and resentments left over from him being a Prince. I am hoping that by seeing what actually happened for the last ten or twelve years, she can get through the old anger and begin preparing for what is happening next."

Burt was intrigued. "Is it normal for women to be angry about the Prince stage? ...*Were you angry with me?*"

"Yes, it is very common." Claudia reached across the table and took his hand. She smiled at him. "But, no, honey, I wasn't angry with you. I understood what was happening and how to deal with it. It was difficult, but it wasn't personal to me. Men don't *do* Prince to make life difficult. *Prince* does *them*."

"I think you need to tell me more about the Prince stage," he said with real interest.

"Certainly, my pleasure!" she said, her smile warming him. "This is the building stage. Being a carpenter, you were building literally. But all men in this stage are building something: their careers; for many, their families; for all, their kingdoms. It is an intense time, completely absorbing, often frustrating, and totally necessary to being a man."

Burt was nodding in agreement. "Ah, yes, I remember that. Nothing in the world was more important than my work and my business. Once I knew I wanted to be a carpenter, it became the center of my world. Even as much as I loved you and the kids, I couldn't stop thinking about it for long. I was always plotting the next contract I wanted to get, or how I wanted to improve my abilities, or whom I wanted to be better than. Years later, it seemed crazy to be that absorbed in work. But at the time, I couldn't do anything else."

Claudia nodded excitedly. "Yes, exactly. That's what I mean by 'Prince does you.' It's not a conscious choice a man makes to be totally absorbed in his career. It is what happens to him in this stage. He is compelled. It's not voluntary. It's not a choice. But most women don't understand that. She thinks her husband or boyfriend is *choosing* to work all the time—and here is the part that hurts her—*instead* of being with her. This is what has her complain about it and resent it."

"I don't remember you complaining. Did *you* resent it?" Burt hoped she didn't. He hadn't meant to hurt her.

"No, honey. I didn't resent it. That's how my upbringing benefited us. I knew you loved us, and I knew you had to work that much. I knew I had a limited amount of your time and attention and I never wasted it complaining. A woman with a Prince has to treat her man like a budget—a tight budget—and spend his time and energy wisely. I would think about what I needed most from you and then ask for it. I trusted that if you *could* provide it, you would."

Burt was nodding his head. He thought again how lucky he had been. "What else did you do when I was in that stage?"

"I tried to give you what you needed. I thought of you like a long distance driver with pit stops. I was the pit crew, as well as your biggest fan. I tried to anticipate what you needed to keep going at full speed, with a full tank of gas and four good tires. Hot dinners, good lunches packed with love, clean socks and underwear, and money set aside for the tools you would need. Practical things like that. And other things too, like special time with the kids, encouragement when you failed, admiration for your achievements, and peace when you got home."

She added with a mischievous smile, "And plenty of sex, of course."

Burt burst out laughing. "Woman, you are amazing!" He couldn't stop laughing, especially with her now trying to look innocent and failing. There was just a little too much twinkle in her eyes. He laughed until tears ran down his cheeks.

He finally stopped laughing and wiped his face with the back of his hand. Then he grew serious. "All that doesn't sound like it was much fun for *you*. Was your life *awful*?" He braced himself for the answer.

She shook her head. "No, honey. My life was difficult sometimes—with two kids, a household, and you to take care of—but it wasn't awful. For one, because I understood what was happening to you and how long it would last. I knew the Prince stage lasts a decade or more. I wasn't hoping for the end everyday. I signed up for the duration, just as you did when you joined the Navy during the War. When you know something is going to last a long time, you can plan. You can strategize—and I did. I made sure I was happy with *my* life. I wanted to be a mother and I enjoyed our kids. I cherished our time together, and I also made the most of you working a lot. That's how our beautiful garden came about. I never gave up that passion and worked on it almost every day."

Burt was relieved. His appreciation for Claudia grew even more.

Claudia continued, "The Prince stage is difficult for everyone. Which, if women knew about it, might make them want to avoid men this age. But there are advantages, too."

"Like what?" He was enjoying this now.

"Well, for example, this is the time when many men are looking for a partner, if that's what they feel they need to build their kingdom. For a woman looking to get married, these men can be much better candidates than the stage before. And when men are Princes, they are like cakes that aren't quite baked. They can be shaped a bit. They'll listen to a woman's advice and recommendations. Also, they have less definitive ideas about what they want to provide, making them more flexible."

"What do you mean by that last part—'definitive ideas about providing'?" He was curious.

"As you know, honey, men are natural providers. It is what they love to do. In the King stage, what they want to provide is narrowly defined; it is limited to certain things. That's not good or bad. There is just what you want to give, and what you don't. In the Prince stage, while their identities are still being developed, men are more open to what the people in their lives need and what will make them happy.

And they often will adapt. I am sure you have heard men this age say something like, 'Sure, honey, whatever will make you happy.' This means a woman has a chance—and a responsibility—to ask a man to provide what she and her children need. This is especially important these days when what is needed is less traditional."

"Say more."

"Well, for many years, men knew that what they needed to provide was money—money to buy food, clothes, shelter, and maybe education. It was simple. Money was what was needed, and men worked to provide it. But now, the needs aren't as simple or as straightforward. A man can't just do what his father did. Unfortunately, he might not know that. He needs his wife to teach him what to provide, by asking him for it, and by valuing it highly."

"Can you give me an example of what that might be? Since I am of the 'bring home the bacon' era, I'm not sure I know what you mean."

Claudia reached across the table and touched his cheek. "It's true, honey, you are of that era. And you did a darn good job of it. Still do, from how you manage our investments. But even then you provided more than that, because I asked. Things like helping Max with his math by showing how it applied to carpentry and making it tangible. Or acting out plays with Myra, reading Romeo so she could be Juliet. Those things were special to them, and to me." Burt swelled with her praise.

"Nowadays, women need to teach men what is important to provide. It is often *not* more money. Especially if she is working, too. But to know what is really needed means she must sort out her priorities. Because, again, a Prince is limited in time and energy. If she concludes that the children need his attention, then that's what she asks him to provide. Afterward, she needs to appreciate it as much as the new raise he got. That's how he learns: by being asked and then being appreciated. Nagging, complaining, and criticizing don't teach him anything."

She paused, reflecting. "This is a different subject, but interesting. Here is another way men and women are different. If you criticize a woman for something, odds are she'll try her darndest never to do it again. She'll never make that meal, never wear that dress, never tell that joke, and never speak up that way again. Criticism doesn't have the same effect on a man. From another man, it's another opinion to consider. From a woman, it just makes him mad and makes him want to provide less."

Claudia sighed. "Anyway, regarding the Stages of Development. The toughest part for any woman, no matter what stage a man is in, is realizing that she can't have it all ways—she can't 'have her cake and eat it too.' In each stage there are things he can do well and things he can't do at all."

As they got up from the table, Burt told Claudia he would do the dishes alone tonight. He was rewarded with a peck on the cheek and a hug. As he cleared the table and loaded the dishwasher, he noticed that he had no fondness, really, for doing dishes. Claudia was right. He did it to *provide* something for her. Some free time, some energy, maybe some fun doing something else.

While he moved around the kitchen, he thought about all those years learning his trade and building his business. He had always known he had an advantage over the single men who had to take care of themselves. At the time, though, he didn't understand why his friends and co-workers often complained about their wives' demands. Now he knew it was because Claudia never made demands, per se. She just taught him what to provide. He could see what he had taken for granted back then: he had always been supported and encouraged by Claudia. Compared to the other married men, she had made his success that much easier to come by.

I always wanted to make her happy, and provide for the kids, he thought. Even while I worked day and night for my business to succeed, not being able to give them enough was the only failure I ever really feared.

Descent Into Darkness

KAREN COULDN'T RELAX UNTIL SHE SAW CLAUDIA ENTER THE YOGA center. Not doubting that Claudia would keep their appointment, she had been anxious nevertheless. After they settled at a corner table in the coffee house, Karen poured out her heart to Claudia.

With the exception of continued, even miraculous progress with Casey in the classroom, it had been a miserable four and a half days. Karen had been unable to talk to Mike about what she had learned last Saturday. When she had told him she couldn't talk about it yet, he had seemed hurt and disappointed, which surprised her. But she was afraid if she started, a torrent of tears and accusations would flood out of her mouth. She didn't want to say something she couldn't take back, especially if Claudia could help her first.

Karen finished telling her everything: losing the ability to blame Mike, all the years of waiting one day at a time, the list of what she really wanted to do. To her surprise, Claudia said, "So you want to know about Princes and children? We don't have to wait until Saturday. I can tell you right now."

Karen sighed with relief. "I just have a feeling that you know what I need to do. When he was a Knight, he kept saying he wasn't ready for kids, and you made me understand that. They would have tied us down and spoiled our adventures. But he's kept saying it. Do you think he really means that he doesn't want kids at all?" She choked on the last sentence.

Claudia got serious. "Look at me."

Karen looked through tears at Claudia. She had never seen her look more intense. Claudia said, "If Mike said he wasn't ready, he meant *he wasn't ready*. Unless pushed into a corner, men say what they mean. If he didn't want children, knowing how much you do, he would have told you a long time ago."

Karen had been holding her breath. Her biggest fear these last few days had been that Mike just didn't want kids. She didn't know what she would do if that were true.

"Remember when we talked about Princes and relationships? I told you that the men seem to fall into two different camps—the group that wants a wife as a partner to help build the kingdom and the group that thinks you build it first, then get a wife. Remember?"

Karen nodded. "I remember."

Claudia leaned forward. "The reason for that has to do with what *providing* means to a man. A man can't get married until he is able to *provide* what he thinks he should. Every man has a different standard. Some Princes think the whole castle should be built before they have any business taking on a wife. Others think they just need the site."

Karen smiled at the metaphor. Claudia continued, "The ones who think they just need the site will usually look for a wife soon after becoming a Middle Prince; soon after they figure out what they want to be King of. The ones who think the whole castle should be built won't be ready to get married until they are a Late Prince, or even after that."

"Okay. I understand that. But what does that have to do with children?"

"The same principle applies to having children. Every man has his own convictions about what children need, and, therefore, what he should be able to *provide* before he has any. If he thinks he can't provide what he should, he will say he isn't ready."

Now Karen was confused. "I don't see how this applies to Mike. We got married when Mike was a Knight. We didn't have anything. He clearly didn't think he had to *provide* something first. Why would he think he has to provide something for children?"

"They are not necessarily the same. It all depends on his perception of his own childhood: what he thought was good and what he still resents not getting. Think about it. Think about what you know about Mike, his family, and his upbringing. If a man wasn't happy with his own childhood, he will want to do better than his own father. Whatever he thought was missing from *his* childhood, he'll want to *provide* for his children. If it was money that was missing, he'll work to provide that. If it's something else, that's what he will focus on. On the other hand, if he is satisfied with his childhood, he will probably think he needs to be able to provide the same things that his parents did."

Karen was dumbstruck; she kept shaking her head. Why haven't I seen this sooner? she thought. Her memory was suddenly reviewing all the conversations she and Mike had had about his childhood over the years. Only this time, connections were being made.

"Oh my gosh," she said. "His parents were immigrants from Italy. They had a big family. His father worked two jobs to support them. Mike's biggest complaint about his childhood has always been *that his father was never home*. Of course—I can't believe I never saw it before."

Now Claudia was shaking her head. Karen could predict what she would say next and laughed a little. "I know, Claudia. I can either beat myself up for not seeing it before or be excited about what is possible now that I have."

Claudia gave her a rare grin. "Well done, Karen," she nodded. "Well done."

"So what do I do now?" Karen asked.

"Obviously, seeing this about Mike lifts your anxiety about the future somewhat. How about the resentment you've felt for waiting all this time? Can you forgive him?"

Boy, Claudia knew how to ask the tough questions. Karen sipped her cappuccino and thought about it. Then something occurred to her. She said suddenly, "That's a trick question!"

Claudia had one of those mysterious smiles again. "Really? How so, dear?"

Karen tried to articulate it. "Well, to forgive him would mean that I thought he had done something to me that he needs to be forgiven for. But, he hasn't done anything to me, has he? You're saying he can't help the standards he has for being a father, right? It is predictable that he would want to have plenty of time for his kids. This is part of what you've been trying to tell me about their sense of self. Right? Part of him*self* is thinking about fatherhood this way. And, I finally understand him," Karen sighed. "Funny, I'm not mad at him anymore. I think it's sweet he would want to be a dad that way."

As she looked closer, she saw tears in Claudia's eyes. "What is it? What's wrong?"

Claudia smiled and shook her head. "There's nothing wrong, dear. I am proud of you."

Now it was Karen's turn to take Claudia's hand. "This is what you meant by 'keys to the kingdom' didn't you?" Claudia nodded. "I thought you were exaggerating when you told me that about your name. But now I believe it. *Thank you for picking me.*"

Claudia squeezed her hand. "You're welcome, my dear. I thank you as well. I need to *give* this to you as much as you need to *receive* it. And it makes my heart fill with joy to see you using it well."

Karen smiled at her until Claudia got up and broke the spell. "I have to go, Karen. At last, you are ready to learn about what is happening to Mike now. I look forward to seeing you on Saturday. Will you make sure to talk to him about Princes before then?"

Karen nodded. "Now that I can talk to him without taking his head off!" She laughed and shook her head. "It terrifies me to think of what I would have said before tonight."

"You were wise to wait. Congratulations on trusting yourself."

Karen looked worried again. "Claudia, I know you have to go, but how should I talk to him about being a father?"

Claudia nodded and sat on the edge of the chair. "Good question. Listen carefully." She paused and smiled. "I apologize. You always listen carefully. It's one of the things I appreciate about you."

She resumed, "There are several things and each is important. Before you talk to him about this, because it is such a sensitive subject for you, make sure you are completely calm. You might do some of your favorite yoga positions and breathe deeply. To be safe for him, you also can't have a correct answer in mind. Set aside what we talked about and what you saw. You must stay open to whatever he says or he won't be able to answer truthfully. When you are ready, say something like, 'I know you haven't been ready to have children. I'm curious—

what do you want to accomplish before you have kids?' Then just listen, without interrupting, like you've been practicing."

When Mike heard Karen pull into the driveway, he tensed. She had been upset the last few days and it was hard to be in the same house with her. Especially since she wouldn't tell him what was wrong. He hated that. He felt doomed. How could he solve the problem if he didn't know what it was?

While his own private hell of doubts had continued as usual, he noticed how much worse they were with Karen upset. The week before, when she had been happy after her first session with Claudia, he'd even started to develop a sense of humor about himself. But this week, with Karen miserable and shutting him out, he had been angry and frustrated all the time.

He knew she was seeing Claudia again tonight, but couldn't bet on the results. So far, it had been fifty/fifty. Which way would it go tonight?

He could tell the difference the moment she entered the room. The light in her face was on. Her eyes shone. Mike breathed a sigh of relief and smiled at her. "Hi, babe. How'd it go?"

Karen smiled back and sat on the couch, turned toward him with her knees gently pressing against his thigh. "It was great. I got exactly what I needed."

"Good. This is good. Do you want to tell me about it?"

Karen nodded and he felt hopeful. After hearing about Pages and Knights, Mike wanted to know more.

"But I want to do a good job of it and I left my notes at school. Could we have, like, a 'date' tomorrow night to talk about it?"

"Sure, why not? Do you want to go somewhere?"

"I don't think so. I'll make dinner and we can hang out at home, okay?"

Mike was a little worried now. Karen usually wanted to go out to dinner. Staying in meant it was a *private* conversation. Was he in trouble?

Karen surprised him by reaching out and taking his hand by the fingers. "You're not in trouble, Mike. I just don't want to be interrupted by some over-attentive waitress."

He relaxed and wondered if she was reading his mind. He looked down and noticed the shape of her breasts under her sweatshirt. His eyes lingered. When he looked up, she was watching him. Did she see that? He didn't have long to wonder.

She tilted her head to the side, the light catching the gold in her eyes. She smiled impishly. "I was wondering…" She touched the top of his thigh with one dainty finger. "Would you be interested in making love with me again?"

He felt a pleasant shock jump up his leg from her finger to his crotch. He grinned. *Jackpot.*

Although she hadn't asked the big question yet, Karen thought she had done a decent job of explaining Princes to Mike. If she were to do it again, she might organize the information a little differently. Always the teacher, modifying the curriculum, she noticed. She wondered if it would be different telling women than it was telling Mike. He wanted all the information, and as they sat over dinner with the candles flickering warmly, he took it in without comment until she was finished. *I guess men listen like they need to be listened to,* she thought. A woman would probably have jumped in, asking questions as she went.

"Well, that's pretty much it," she concluded. "Does any of that apply to you?"

Mike nodded and took a sip of his wine. Dinner was now finished, but still sitting on the table. They hadn't moved for more than an hour. It was nice.

"It definitely applies to me. And I can see how it applies to the men on the crew, too. I've had lots of guys come on when they were Early Princes. For some, the work fit, and they stayed. For others, you could tell it wasn't really their thing. I knew they wouldn't last long.

I've also lost good men because I couldn't advance them. They got to the point where they had learned everything they could from me and had to move on. I was sorry to lose them, but I understood."

He continued, "I don't think I was an Early Prince for long. Maybe a minute. I guess it's because I tried a lot of things when I was a Knight, chasing after fun and challenge. In Zimbabwe, I found my niche. When we got back, I knew what I wanted and just went for it."

Karen nodded slightly and kept listening. It felt good to know he saw it the same way she did. She was surprised by what he said about his crew, though. Seems like this information could help in business too, she thought.

"It helps to hear what Claudia said about being 'compelled.' I knew you wanted me to work less and be at home more, but I just couldn't. When I tried to, I got antsy. It felt wrong. I could practically feel the opportunities I was missing. It was frustrating. I had to work, even when it made you mad. If I didn't, it made me mad, and that was worse."

Ah, she thought. That's how it worked. Tough choice. Terrible choice. If only I had known…Stop, Karen. Keep your promise to Claudia.

Mike was silent. Karen waited. Finally, it seemed like he had made up his mind about something. He looked at her tentatively. "Can I tell you something?" She nodded. "Try not to get mad, okay?" She nodded again.

"In the beginning, you were really supportive. You encouraged me. You told me I was smart. You believed in me. I needed that. And you helped me get my office set up, remember? Sometimes you even pretended you were my secretary and returned calls when I was at the site and couldn't—in the days before almost everyone had a cell phone. It was great. And little things: You packed me lunch and put little notes in it. You bragged about me to your parents. That made me proud."

He paused. "What changed, Karen? Did it just grow old?"

Karen gulped. "I think the problem was that I didn't understand it. I thought once the novelty of your business wore off, you would be home more, and you would talk about something else. I thought you would be more interested in what I was doing. I didn't know it was a stage. And I had no idea it would last a decade."

She could feel her eyes tearing up. "I'm sorry, Mike. I'm sorry for not supporting you. I wasn't getting what I needed, and I stopped wanting to give you anything." She gulped again. "I thought you weren't giving me what I needed because you didn't want to. Because you didn't care about me." She sighed, "I didn't know that you couldn't."

Mike reached over and took her hand. He looked miserable. "What did you need, babe?"

Karen looked in his eyes. "I needed your attention. I needed you to be proud of me, too. And I needed things that weren't fair to expect, I know now. I needed you to complete me, because I gave up too much of myself."

"What do you mean?" He looked perplexed. He let go of her hand.

"Claudia told me that a woman's strength is in her ability to adapt, but the downside is that we adapt so much we literally lose ourselves. She says women have to keep their individual passions alive, or we forget who we are. Something like that happened to me."

Mike was quiet, thinking. Karen counted silently, determined not to interrupt. After awhile, he spoke. "I *was* proud of you. But in the beginning I couldn't show it because I was afraid. For a long time, you were doing better as a teacher than I was as a contractor. I felt competitive. When you talked about how well your job was going, I tried to be happy for you, but I just felt bad for myself. It made me worry that I wasn't good enough. And, soon after that, your teaching became your priority. I had to wait in line to get what I needed from you. It didn't exactly make me love your students or your committees."

Karen was amazed. It had only just occurred to her that speaking while he was thinking would also interrupt him. With her being silent and waiting, Mike had dug even deeper. Fascinating. She was learning as much from Mike as from Claudia. Did Claudia intend this? It wouldn't surprise her.

Mike seemed finished and Karen decided to comment. "I never thought of it that way. I got tired of waiting for you and I immersed myself in my work. I think it was to divert my attention from how hurt I felt. A vicious cycle, huh?"

Mike nodded and took her hand again. "I'm sorry. I never meant for you to feel neglected. When I got paid on a contract, I always thought of what I'd be able to get for you. I wanted you to have a lot of things that I couldn't give you. It seemed if I just worked harder, then I could give you everything and make you happy."

Karen was touched and saddened. What a waste. If only she had known. "I've learned a lot from Claudia about what I could have done differently. Like using the limited amount of attention you could pay me wisely. I wasted it on complaining about how little attention you gave me. Silly, huh? There is so much I wish I knew then. And I can see how other couples are bound to suffer from what they don't understand."

She decided to take the plunge. She took a deep breath, just like she was taught in yoga, and consciously relaxed her body.

"Can I ask you a question, Mike?"

"Sure."

"For a long time, you've said that you weren't ready to have children. I am only now beginning to understand what that means. What do you need to accomplish before having kids?" She bit her lip while she waited for his answer. When she noticed, she breathed in again and calmed herself.

Mike was silent. She waited, letting go of everything she hoped he would say, and everything she was afraid he would say. Finally, after what seemed an eternity, he answered.

"Honestly, right now, I don't know."

Karen felt a groan and suppressed it. This was not one of the possible answers! She could be right about "more time" or wrong about "more time." If she were wrong about him wanting more time for his kids, then it would be something else he needed. Fine. She could deal with whatever it was. For Mike to not know meant there was still nothing she could do about it. Ugh.

Fortunately, she said nothing and kept listening.

Mike spoke again, "Whenever you ask me about kids, I picture us having three or four of them. And I've always wanted that. In my mind, they look like you. They're beautiful."

Tears sprang to Karen's eyes. She tried blinking them away.

"But then I had to look at it realistically. For much of the last decade, I've left for work at dawn. I'd get back an hour or more after sunset, depending on how far away the job was, and how bad traffic was. Usually, I still had work to do in my office. Preparing invoices, ordering materials, paying bills. You know how late I worked. What would be left? When would I see them? When would they see me? I don't want to be like my father. I want to give them more. I want to give them more of myself."

Karen kept calm, her hands clasped in her lap.

Mike continued, "That's what I've thought for a long time, for years even. But now, my business is stable. The money is steady and it doesn't take as much time. Honestly, I am not nearly as interested in my work as I have been. But I am still not ready to have kids. Only now, there is this terrible feeling of unease, for no concrete reason."

Mike offered his hand to her, palm up, on the table. She took it and looked up at him. She couldn't suppress the tears that flowed down her cheeks, and she could barely swallow around the lump in her throat.

He squeezed her fingers tightly. "Honey, I don't know what's wrong with me. I'm in such a funky place. I know how much you want kids. Please, just give me a little more time. Okay?"

Karen sighed. She thought of Claudia and the session coming up and managed to say, "Claudia told me that this Saturday she is going to tell me about the stage you are in now. Let's just hope it doesn't last ten to fifteen years like the other ones." She tried to joke, smiling a little through her sadness.

Mike reached over and carefully wiped away her tears. He cupped her jaw gently in his big, rough hand. "Claudia has helped us both already. I'm sure whatever she has to say next will be just as good."

Karen stood and they hugged. Oh God, let that be true.

Burt answered the door and let Karen in. Karen seemed a bit flustered and he tried to put her at ease.

"Claudia will be back any moment, Karen. She just made a quick trip to the store for some cocoa. Seems to her like a good day for hot chocolate, what with the weather turning chilly. What do you think?"

"I think every day is a good day for chocolate, in any form," said Karen with a smile.

As Burt chuckled in response, he noticed Karen leaning toward the mantle. "Would you like to look at the pictures?" he asked, since she obviously wanted to.

Burt gave Karen a guided tour of the family pictures on the mantle, walls, and sideboard. "This is me in my uniform after I joined the Navy. This is our wedding picture. We got married when I was on leave for a couple of weeks. Doesn't Claudia look lovely? This is little Max. He was born while I was at sea. That was hard for Claudia, but it happened a lot during the War."

Karen seemed interested, so he kept going. "This is our first house. Just a little bungalow was all I could afford. Since then, we've never left Pasadena. Claudia loves it here. That's the house where Myra was born. Here she is. Look at those eyes—serious, even as a baby."

He picked up a picture of which he was especially proud. "This is Claudia when she received her degree in anthropology. Back then it was highly unusual for forty-year-old married women to go to college. She loved it." He picked up another picture. "This is Claudia at the Chamber of Commerce. She was getting an award for outstanding service."

Karen seemed surprised. "Claudia worked for the Chamber of Commerce?"

Burt chuckled. "Oh, yes. After she finished her degree, she said there was no better place to study men. There and the Veteran's Administration, where she volunteered."

Finished with the photo tour, Burt suggested Karen wait for Claudia in the garden. He escorted her out and showed her the lap blanket she could use if she got cold. Then he made his way to his shop, rubbing his hands together in anticipation of the wood calling to him.

Waiting idly for Claudia, Karen had a chance to examine the table where they always sat. The surface of the round table was smooth except for about three inches around the outer edge, which were carved in what Karen had assumed was a floral pattern. As she looked more closely at the rich, dark wood she saw the carvings for what they were. Instead of flowers, they were faces. About three inches by three inches each, there were at least twenty different carvings bordering the table. From the pictures she had just seen inside, she immediately recognized the face: Claudia laughing, Claudia smiling, Claudia pursing her lips in thought. Claudia looking serene, Claudia looking mischievous—even Claudia sleeping. The faces were of different ages, young and old and in-between, but they were all of Claudia.

So engrossed was she in the table, Karen had worked her way around the other side and didn't see Claudia entering the garden. She was startled when Claudia came up beside her and said, "Hello, dear. I see you have discovered my table."

Karen looked at the table and then back at Claudia in wonder. It was more than Burt's obvious talent that amazed her.

As if reading her mind, Claudia smiled humbly. "Yes, it's true. He adores me."

Speechless, Karen sat down in her usual seat, noticing that the armrests held little Claudia carvings, too.

Claudia set down the two mugs she was carrying and watched Karen. The table never failed to amaze the people who discovered it. Burt's talent for carving was very special, but it was the subject matter that opened up a new world for people. A world of unimaginable love and devotion. This table and two chairs were her Taj Mahal.

In the ten years since Burt had made them for her, Claudia had been fascinated by people's reactions. What was most interesting to her was *when* they noticed the carvings. There were family members and neighbors who had been in their backyard numerous times without ever really seeing the table and chairs. It was as if the carvings were invisible.

Her theory was that seeing them required an open heart. Claudia took it as a good omen that Karen had seen the table today.

She smiled, ready to begin. "How are you, my dear?"

Karen smiled back; was she blushing? "I'm good, Claudia. Really good."

Sensing there was more, Claudia asked, "Do you want to tell me about it?"

Karen *was* blushing. She blurted, "Mike and I have been making love a lot more than usual. And a lot…better than usual." She tried to cover her embarrassment by taking a sip of hot chocolate; she licked the whipped cream from her upper lip.

Claudia smiled gently. "That's perfectly understandable."

"It is? How so?"

"Well," Claudia said, "you've been seeing Mike in a new light, creating a special, good kind of distance that causes excitement. And you have been understanding him, creating intimacy. Distance and intimacy, the perfect combination for great sex."

Karen laughed. "You know about sex, too?"

Claudia smiled, realizing it must be difficult to talk about this with someone much older. "You can't understand men without understanding sex as well. It was part of my education."

"No stone unturned, huh?" Karen asked.

"Something like that. Over the years my ancestors developed an extensive body of knowledge covering the everyday workings of men. That's required learning for each new generation. Some of us continue to study along those lines and some of us head off in other directions."

"While I was waiting for you, Burt told me that you worked for the Chamber of Commerce and volunteered at the VA in order to study men. What is *your* area? Did you stick with the basics or 'head off'? If you don't mind my asking."

Claudia was pleased. She didn't mind Karen asking; in fact, it was delightful. She had been studying men with no one with whom to share it. "I headed off, as I always knew I would. My fascination is with the paradoxes of men. That is what I have been spending most of my time on."

Karen took another sip from her mug. "This cocoa is delicious. What do you mean by the paradoxes?"

"Well, for example, the paradox of loyalty and competition—they co-exist in men. Like violence and a craving for peace. Like the fact that a man can be ready to kill another man, or be willing to die for him. Those paradoxes."

"Can you tell me more?" Karen asked, sounding hopeful.

"Someday, maybe; I'm not done studying them. And, anyway, we have an important topic today, as I am sure you remember." She smiled at Karen.

Karen smiled back. "Yep, I sure do. And I did my homework. Mike and I had a great talk about being a Prince. We talked about what it was like for him and what it was like for me. I sure learned a lot from listening to him. But I bet you knew that would happen."

Claudia was delighted. "We always learn a lot from men whenever we're willing to listen. And especially when we are able to hear."

Karen leaned her head to the side. "What do you mean, 'able to hear'?"

Claudia loved how Karen picked up on these nuances, and how ready she was to learn. "Karen, I am sure that the things Mike told you this week, he has told you before. Perhaps many times. Men are always telling us what they need and what they think; to do this is part of their nature. But we are not always able to hear them. Because we assume they communicate like women, we're always looking for some deeper, hidden meaning. We miss their communication because we can't take it at face value. Part of what is happening from our time together is that you are becoming able to *hear* Mike."

Claudia let that sink in. "You are doing well, Karen. Better than I hoped." Karen smiled, pleased at the compliment.

"Are you ready?" Claudia asked.

"Yes! I finally get to hear about the stage Mike is in, right?" Karen said and reached for her pad and pen.

Claudia adjusted the lap blanket and warmed her hands on her mug. She prepared herself for possibly the most difficult lesson yet. Karen was poised, pen in hand. "Mike is not really in a stage, Karen.

That is the difficulty. Mike is in the transition between Prince and King and it is extremely uncomfortable."

"What do you mean?"

"After being a Late Prince for a while, a man enters a transition period. We call it the Tunnel. You could think of it as a cocoon. On the other side he will be as transformed as the caterpillar that turns into a butterfly. But it is an extremely uncomfortable cocoon. It was once labeled, 'The Descent into Darkness.'"

"That sounds awful. What does it mean?"

"They called it that because with each step a man takes in the Tunnel, he becomes less certain about who he is and what he knows to be true. His identity is profoundly in question. In fact, that is what rules this transition period. Questions, questions, questions. He will involuntarily question everything. What is important to him, his standards, and the value of all that he spent a decade building. Nothing is off limits.

"But the questions don't bring answers. Just more questions. That is the torture. Men are compelled to solve problems and they always solve them consistent with their values, consistent with themselves. The Tunnel is one long string of unsolvable problems. They can't be solved because the basis for solving them—his sense of self—is in question. He is standing on quicksand and he can't move in any direction."

"Is that why Mike is frustrated and angry all the time?"

"Yes. What makes it worse is that Late Princes are characterized by a growing certainty and confidence. It's all coming together. It's wonderful. Then one morning they wake up and it begins falling apart. Out of nowhere, they are suddenly being plagued by doubts. You can imagine how that might be for a man. They often wonder if they are going crazy."

"Sometimes Mike sounds like he's crazy. And he hates what he is like." Karen paused, considering. Quietly she asked, "Does being in the Tunnel affect their sex drive?"

Claudia kept her face blank for Karen's sake. "Yes, dear. But it's not predictable. Some men lose interest in sex. Others need much more of it."

Karen seemed satisfied. "When does the Tunnel start? Is it at a certain age? Mike is 42—is that normal?"

Claudia could see Karen making connections. More importantly, she could see the compassion she was starting to feel for Mike. Compassion is appropriate for Tunnel-men, she thought.

"The Tunnel doesn't start at a particular age as much as at a particular time. It seems to begin about ten to thirteen years after a man becomes a Middle Prince. In other words, a little more than a decade after he has identified the site of his kingdom and gotten seriously to work. When the Tunnel happens age-wise depends on how young he became an Early Prince and how long it took him to find the career or work that fit him. I know of men who entered the Tunnel as early as 35, but that is unusual. They were very serious, even in college, and knew exactly what they wanted to do. If a man becomes a Middle Prince at twenty-eight, he'll enter the Tunnel between thirty-eight and forty-one, roughly. I know a man who didn't identify his kingdom until he was thirty-five. He entered the Tunnel at forty-eight. As you can see, it all depends on the man and the circumstances."

Karen was counting on her fingers. "We came back from Zimbabwe when I was twenty-seven and Mike was thirty. He just turned forty-two last month. As far as I can tell, he's been in the Tunnel for about eight months. That's when all the fun ended and the fights began. Does that sound right?"

Claudia nodded. "He's right on track. And at a typical age, too. He must get teased a lot about having a mid-life crisis."

"How'd you guess? People say that's why he bought his red Miata convertible."

Claudia frowned. "Unfortunately, almost no one understands the Tunnel. Least of all, women. I think we call it a mid-life crisis because it *is* a crisis—for us."

Karen leaned forward in her chair. "I know it has felt that way for me. Why is that?"

"Because it is a one-man Tunnel, Karen. A man must go through it alone. It only works that way. There is no room in that cocoon for anyone else. And if there were, he would fail to come out. Therefore, the process of the Tunnel causes a man to distance himself from everyone else. Especially those most important to him. This distance drives women crazy. We are biologically dependent upon feeling connected. The Tunnel threatens that."

Karen held up her hand. "Wait a second; you just said a mouthful. I gotta take this one piece at a time. What do you mean 'biologically dependent'?"

Claudia sighed. "It's kind of off the subject. Suffice it to say that as women we have depended upon our connections to other people to keep us alive. For ages, we needed other people to survive. How we know that they will come through for us is by how connected we feel. When we don't feel connected, especially to a man, romantically, we panic. It is an ancient survival reaction. We mostly respond to it without thinking, seeking intimacy anywhere we can find it."

She paused. "The real problem is that the way most women approach a man in the Tunnel makes intimacy impossible. Sometimes we can feel like we are free falling and it's frightening. That is what makes the Tunnel a crisis for us."

Karen's brown eyes were round and wide. "Wow." Claudia waited and let that piece of information get situated for Karen.

Finally, Karen asked, "What did you mean by a man having to distance himself especially from those most important to him?"

Claudia took a deep breath. "Remember last week when we talked about men and their sense of self?" Karen nodded.

"When a man is a Knight or a Prince, his sense of self comes partly from within, and partly from his activities, his friends, his family, and his girlfriend or wife. Who *he* thinks he is has been shaped in part by who *they* think he is. In the Tunnel, he has to distance himself from those closest to him, those who most shape his identity. This leaves him free to create his identity strictly within himself. That is what the Tunnel is all about. He is questioning all the influences he has experienced and deciding who he is existentially." Claudia stopped and looked at Karen. "Are you alright, dear? I know this is a lot to accept and it is close to home."

"It just hurts. I think if he loved me more, he wouldn't shut me out."

Claudia sighed. "I know it seems that way. Like he is shutting *you* out. But it doesn't happen like that; the Tunnel forces him to go it alone. This is one of the keys to the kingdom: knowing what not to take personally so you're not hurt by things he can't control."

Karen looked up at her with a mixture of hope and concern. "How long does it last, Claudia? And what happens on the other side?"

Claudia held Karen's gaze in sympathy. "On the other side he will become a King. And I have much to teach you about that stage. Kings are a very different kind of man than anything that comes before. New rules apply. But we have plenty of time for that."

She took a sip of her hot chocolate. "As to how long it lasts, that depends. It seems to take between six months and three years. The average is somewhere in the middle and some men don't come out at all."

Karen looked shocked. "Really? They don't come out at all? Why is that?"

Claudia pursed her lips, thinking about how much she should say. "It requires a tremendous amount of courage to come out of the Tunnel. The courage to literally define oneself and say 'to hell' with anyone who doesn't like it. Not all men can do it. I am not sure why. No one in my ancestry has studied that phenomenon extensively."

She continued, "For those who do come out, which is most of them, how long it takes seems to depend on what they do while they are in it. There are some things we have seen that can speed up the process."

Claudia thought Karen was going to jump out of her seat. "Really, really? What are they?"

"Okay, okay," Claudia laughed. "Mind you, they don't all work for everyone and some are more conventional than others."

She continued, "The most tried and true are on opposite ends of the spectrum. On the one hand is someone a Tunnel-man can talk to as a sounding board. It needs to be someone who doesn't offer opinions or judgments, and just listens while he talks it all out. All his questions. All his wonderings. Then he can get them out of his head and out in front of him. These days the right type of therapist might provide something like that. Or a coach or a consultant."

"What is on the other end of the spectrum?"

"A defining moment. This is the opposite of something safe and slow like a friend to talk to. This is something that forces a man's hand. Not as easy to arrange, since they usually involve a crisis or emergency. I don't recommend it."

Claudia waited while Karen filled in her notes. "You said those were more tried and true. What else is there?" Karen asked.

"There are a couple of things I heard about when I worked at the Chamber of Commerce. I took the job because I knew it would afford many opportunities to observe men and talk to men. I needed more than just Burt and Max and their friends to study. It was rich. Among other things, over the years I watched several men go through the Tunnel. I noticed some men who seemed to make it through faster and I found out they had taken a couple of 'new age' programs."

Claudia waited to see how Karen would respond. Some teachers were open to all types of learning; others were more conventional and everything had to be credentialed. Since Karen was willing to learn from her, she thought Karen was the more open type, but she remembered what Burt had said about giving advice to folks who don't ask for it.

Karen said, "I think Mike is pretty open-minded. The Peace Corps certainly exposed us to lots of different philosophies. What are the programs?"

Claudia smiled and proceeded. "I'll tell you about them, but be careful not to recommend them to Mike. You can tell him about them if he asks, but don't suggest he do them, okay? Remember, safe, safe, safe. Never suggest anything."

Karen nodded. "Okay. I'll be careful."

"One company I heard about is called Landmark Education. They have something called the Landmark Forum and a follow-up class they call the Advanced Course. One gentleman I observed said he did both. When I asked him about them, he said the first one helped him to free himself of his past limitations. He said the advanced one gave him a way to re-create himself. Sounded perfect to me, since that is what a Tunnel-man has to do. Burt helped me look it up on the Internet. I think they are all over the place. It looks interesting."

"You said there were two programs. What is the other one?"

"The other one is called the New Warrior Training Adventure."

"Warrior? Sounds strange. What is it?"

"It seems to help men come to terms with their manhood by creating a right of passage. This is very important nowadays, when manliness is often suppressed. The man I knew who went through it came back to work powerful and at peace with himself. I noticed the difference right way. After that, he was done with the Tunnel and on his way. I don't know if it affects all men that way, but what I saw was exciting. They're on the Internet, too."

"It sure would be great if Mike did something like this."

Claudia sipped her cocoa. "Well, we don't know yet if he will or not. Let's talk about what *you* can do. At least *that* you can control."

"What *can* I do?" Karen looked hopeful. Too hopeful, Claudia thought. Better warn her.

"Karen, as I tell you what you can do, you are likely to see mistakes you've been making. Are you prepared for that?"

Karen sighed. "I figure by now that it comes with the territory. At least I won't have to *keep* making them."

Once again, Claudia was impressed by Karen. Sure is a deep well of courage in this young woman, she thought.

"The Tunnel is an extraordinary, intense, soul-searching time for a man. One thing you can do to support him is to honor the process he is in. You might consider it a sacred time in a man's life. I do."

Claudia paused. "When I say 'support,' I mean it in a different way than the support you provided when Mike was a Prince. Princes will listen to and even seek advice. That would be a mistake with Mike now. Don't advise him. Don't tell him what *you* think is important." Claudia paused as she saw the stricken look on Karen's face.

"Oh, dear. I've been doing a lot of that."

"That's understandable. Just stop. Maybe apologize. What Mike needs the most from you is what I have been having you practice for two weeks now. Just listen and listen and listen."

"Gosh, has it only been two weeks? It's made a big difference. But is that all? Is there anything else?"

"Yes: *Be his friend.* This is another key to the kingdom. When we are someone's friend, we listen to them and their lives in a concerned but detached sort of way. Because what is happening to them doesn't affect our lives. With husbands or boyfriends we tend to listen like everything will have an effect on us. That makes us very *attached* and not safe to talk to. It makes us a lousy friend, because we are mostly concerned with ourselves, not them. Pretend Mike is your friend and just care about him."

"That's hard to do since his life does affect mine. Every day."

Claudia nodded. "I know, dear. That is where it gets tricky. You will have to trust that everything is going to turn out and stop trying to control it. Stop trying to hold on to the life you knew, and the Mike you knew, and trust the process he is in. Trust Mike. Men have the darndest way of turning into the men they were meant to be. And I'll bet that a long time ago you fell in love with the man Mike is going to be. Trust that. And relax."

Karen looked at her with tears in her eyes. "Okay, I think I can do that. Is there anything else I can do?"

Claudia smiled. "These are the most important things. Be a friend. And listen. Beyond that, don't make fun of him and don't let anyone else make fun of him."

"Okay. I think I can get through this."

Claudia raised her mug as if to make a toast. "There is an upside, you know."

Karen looked surprised. "Really? What?"

Claudia sipped her cocoa. "I think you have started to experience it. If you practice being safe to talk to, by listening a lot without judgment or interruption, the level of intimacy can become extraordinary, even priceless. A man is vulnerable in this transition. If you are safe for him, he may show you his soul."

When Burt returned from the lumberyard, he found Claudia lying on the couch with her eyes closed. He went to her side and touched her hand. She opened her eyes. "Hello, sweetheart," she said slowly.

"Are you okay, honey?"

She rolled to her side and pulled the lap blanket up higher. "I'm just tired. I was picking up after Karen left and the couch and the blanket became an irresistible combination." She smiled sleepily.

"How about I make us some dinner and then, if you feel like it, you can tell me about it?"

Claudia nodded. "That would be perfect."

Burt went to the kitchen and started making dinner. Since he could tell Claudia needed to nap awhile, he wasn't in any hurry. He made them soup and grilled cheese sandwiches, his specialty. When everything was ready, he peeked in at Claudia. She hadn't moved at all. Instead of getting her up, he found the TV trays and quietly set them up in front of the couch. After bringing all the food and utensils in from the kitchen, he sat down at her feet and watched her sleep. She looked peaceful, like an angel. I think she is an angel, he thought. My angel. Maybe Karen's angel, too.

Claudia must have felt him watching her because she stirred and opened her eyes. When she saw the trays and food, she grinned. She sat up with more enthusiasm than he expected.

"I'm famished!" she said and picked up her sandwich.

"This work you are doing with Karen sure makes you hungry," he commented. "You were starving last Saturday, too."

Claudia smiled at him in between bites. "Strange, isn't it? I usually eat more like a bird. It takes a lot of energy to teach. It's harder than I thought it would be."

"What makes it that way, do you think?" he asked as he picked up his spoon. Ah, tomato soup at the first chill of fall. He loved that.

"I think it's because what I am teaching is different from the way the world sees men. It's like I have to plow through all the misinformation to clear a path for this. And Karen has to, too. I can see in her face how almost everything I say challenges what she has assumed to be true."

She took a spoonful of her soup. "It's inspiring though, how willing she is to give it all up. I guess she's had enough misery to show her that it didn't serve her. I think she is more exhausted than I am. She has to reconcile her whole life with what I'm telling her. At least I am accustomed to these ideas."

"Do you want to tell me what you talked about today?"

She didn't answer immediately. He ate and waited.

"Actually," she said, "it would help me if I could tell you what I forgot to tell Karen. Then it might stop bothering me."

"Sure, honey. What stage were you on today?"

"Remember when I told you that Mike isn't actually in a stage, that he is in a transition?"

"Yes, but you didn't say much about it. Does it come after the Prince stage?"

Claudia nodded. "Yes, it's the transition from Prince to King. But it's not a 'greased slide' as they say. It is really difficult. We call it the Tunnel."

"The Tunnel? Is this something a man goes into?" Burt asked, and Claudia nodded. "What makes a man go into the Tunnel?" He was curious.

"Usually it's a combination of accomplishments and time. Almost every man I have known falls into the Tunnel a dozen years after he starts building in earnest. He feels really accomplished and eases up, enjoying life more. He's really confident and certain. That's what we call Late Prince. It usually lasts about six months or more before the Tunnel begins. But sometimes nature forces it early, like in your case."

Burt was surprised. "What do you mean?"

"When you returned from the War it took you a while to figure out what you wanted to do. You would try one thing and then another, sure they were going to be it, but they weren't."

Burt nodded. "Yep. I thought I should use the engineering I learned in the Navy as a career. But I hated being indoors all the time. And paper doesn't qualify as wood. I missed working with my hands."

"Since you started your formal training in your trade when you were twenty-nine, I expected you to enter the Tunnel when you were forty-one or forty-two. By the time you turned forty, you had a lot of accomplishments but you weren't talking yet like a Late Prince. You hadn't started to relax and have more time for other things. When I would ask, there were still many things you thought you needed to accomplish. I thought the Tunnel was still a ways off."

Burt was nodding, remembering. Then it struck him. "And then my dad died." It still pained him to think of it, even many years later.

Claudia nodded. "And you fell into the Tunnel headlong, overnight."

Burt scratched his cheek. "Why do you think that is?"

"I think it is nature's way of dealing with the death of the King. It creates a vacuum, so to speak. He needs to be replaced, and that pulls the son right in and hurries up the process. You spent only a short time in the Tunnel—only four or five months. It's as if you weren't allowed to linger there."

"Do you think that always happens when a man's father dies?"

She shrugged. "I'm not sure. If a man is too young, it won't put him in the Tunnel. On the other hand, if a man were close enough, his father wouldn't necessarily have to die. He might just get sick, or something else that causes the son to come face to face with his father's mortality."

Burt was fascinated by the subject but he wanted to make sure Claudia got what she needed. "Is this what you forgot to tell Karen today? Is this what was bothering you?"

"That was the first part. It is just a matter of covering all the bases. I'm pretty sure it doesn't apply to her husband, though. I think he arrived at the Tunnel more normally." She finished her soup. "The other part I forgot to tell her was about fast cars and the mid-life crisis."

"Is there a connection? Do men buy fast cars when they're in the Tunnel? How come I didn't get one?" he teased.

She laughed. "You didn't get one because there isn't a connection. There only seems to be a connection. That's why men get made fun of. And yours was a new truck, anyhow."

"Alright, now you've really got to explain yourself." When she was feisty like this, it made him want to tickle her. He reached over with a knobby finger and lightly prodded her ribs. She giggled and squirmed, which made his day.

"How can I explain myself when you are tickling me?" she pretended to chastise him. "There's no connection between the two; it's just a coincidence of timing. It goes like this: a man falls in love with a sports car or a classic car, or in your case, a truck, when he is younger. He wants one just like that, but he can't afford it. He's got mouths to feed and shoes to buy and tuitions to fund, and most men are responsible about those obligations. So, he goes without. Then, as a Late Prince, he has many accomplishments and more resources than before. Often, this occurs around the time the children go out on their own. More resources with fewer demands on them. Finally, he can afford the car he has wanted for fifteen or twenty years—and he buys it. Shortly after that he falls into the Tunnel, and starts questioning everything and acting strangely, and people think they are connected. They think his so-called 'mid-life crisis' caused him to want the car. But it's inaccurate. He has wanted that car for years and he finally got it. Timing, yes, but no connection. I think he should be congratulated, not be the butt of jokes." Claudia looked pleased with herself.

"And was this important to tell Karen?" he asked, trying to sound serious.

"Absolutely. Mike bought a Miata and folks are teasing him about it. Completely unacceptable!" She tried to look indignant but couldn't hold it; she ended up laughing at herself. Burt was having a great time.

Then she grew more serious. "I love Tunnel-men. This not-a-stage stage is my favorite."

"Why is that?"

"Because women have no natural equivalent and because Tunnel-men are darn cute."

Burt laughed. "Cute? These men are 'cute'?"

Claudia nodded. "Every stage is characterized by some particular, dominant feature that gives men in that stage a certain air about them. For Knights it's adventure, which makes them sexy; for Princes it's building, which makes them very serious; and for Kings it's providing, which gives them weight and stature. For Tunnel-men, it's questions, wonderings and doubts. I think it makes them cute. Unless of course, you are trying to get them to commit to something; then it makes them infuriating."

Burt chuckled. Tunnel-men were clearly her favorite. She even said "infuriating" like she thought that was cute too.

"What did you mean by 'women have no equivalent'? Don't women go through the stages, too, and hit the Tunnel?"

Claudia was shaking her head; then she nodded.

"Which one is it?" Burt asked.

"It's both, actually. Women don't go through stages, not as women. Because we are not linear like men. We are everything we can be from the beginning and just naturally develop whatever parts of ourselves we use. We can develop new capacities at any time, at any age." She paused. "On the other hand, if women are deeply involved in the workplace, they can become masculinized, and may feel like they are going through stages. I haven't studied it, but I don't think they have a Tunnel waiting for them. The Tunnel is ancient and women being this involved in the workplace, isolated from family, is a relatively new phenomenon."

"How come you never became masculine? You worked for a long time."

Claudia beamed at him. "When I was at work, I was masculine, when that's what was needed. I could be feminine too, though, and it was very effective. Remember a couple of weeks ago, when I first met Karen, and we talked about Transition Time?"

Burt nodded, remembering. "Yes, what about it?"

"I always made sure to use a Transition Ritual after work to return me to my femininity. I didn't want to be masculine at home. I would have been butting heads with you and Max all the time. I used a Transition Ritual to make sure I wasn't."

"What kind of ritual do you mean? Like the way I put my keys away and check through the mail and change my clothes?"

Claudia nodded. "Something like that. Only I would pick the ritual that shifted me back into the type of femininity I wanted. I have different rituals depending upon which aspect of myself I want to express."

"Can you tell me more about it, or is it a female secret?" he asked, half hoping she wouldn't tell. He liked her being a mystery.

Claudia smiled knowingly. "Don't worry, it won't ruin anything for you. Femininity is so powerful for men that even understanding it doesn't change that. To put it in simplified terms, I have a different ritual for when I want to be playful or sexual, another for when I need to be nurturing, and another for when being visionary or generous or serene is called for."

Burt was amazed. He had no idea that Claudia had such control over herself. No wonder she was influential. And her explanation made her no less mysterious.

Lying spent on his back, Mike pulled Karen closer, enjoying the feel of her skin against his. He sighed peacefully. "So, I'm not going crazy, huh?"

She reached up and nuzzled his neck. "Nope, I guess not. Are you disappointed?" she teased gently. He loved how throaty her voice sounded after they made love.

"Ha! No way."

He thought about it. How do I feel? "I'm relieved. I thought I was losing it." He leaned his head down to smell her hair. "How come no one knows about this Tunnel thing? It's bad enough going through it; not knowing what's happening to you makes it a living hell."

He felt her squeeze him tightly. "That's what I think about everything Claudia tells me: how come no one knows this? It's a shame. It could help so many people."

Mike held her and thought about the last couple of weeks. Who *is* Claudia, really? he wondered. When Karen first told him about her, he was understandably skeptical. What was her background? Her education? Her qualifications? Now he didn't care. The proof is in the pudding, he thought. How true. He felt more connected to Karen than he had in years. And through her information, Claudia had turned a terrible and confusing part of his life into something interesting and worthwhile.

Well, mostly, he thought. There was still a major glitch. He knew Karen needed to have children, and soon, both from a physical and emotional standpoint. He wanted to give them to her, but just couldn't. Not yet.

"Babe? Are you awake?"

"Uh huh," she murmured against him.

"Did Claudia tell you anything that helps a man get through the Tunnel? Talking about it is good, but is there anything else?" He might have imagined it, but he thought he felt her stop breathing for a moment.

She responded, her head still resting on his chest, "She told me about a couple of classes. I could leave you the websites if you want to check them out."

"Cool."

I Y'am What I Y'am

WEDNESDAY WAS BECOMING KAREN'S FAVORITE DAY. CASEY STAYED after school to help her fix up the classroom, or grade papers, or anything else she could find. It was fun for both of them. She brought a snack and it felt like their own little work party. She was practicing listening with Casey, too. She didn't finish his sentences and she didn't prompt him when he didn't answer right away; she just kept listening and waited. He had become quite the talker and it was delightful. She was also surprised by how bright and interesting he had become. Or maybe always had been?

Wednesday night after yoga class she spent time with Claudia at the coffee house and reported in. It was fun, and not as stressful as their Saturday sessions. Karen couldn't believe it had been only a little more than three weeks since she had spotted Claudia in yoga as a new student. She remembered the tingling she had felt when their eyes first met. Some premonition, she thought. *I guess a part of me knew she was going to change my life.*

Karen insisted on treating Claudia to a gourmet hot chocolate. "It is the least I can do," she said. "Mike is much calmer since he found out he's right on track. It makes the questions and doubts more bearable, he says. Now they have a purpose."

Claudia just smiled, as if that was to be expected. Then Karen told Claudia about Mike's answer to last week's question, "What do you need to accomplish before having children?"

Claudia was sympathetic. "Don't worry, dear. He'll figure it all out soon, I am sure. And besides, there are many advantages to having children with a King."

"What do you mean?" Karen was curious. Could there be a silver lining?

"Men approach fatherhood differently depending on what stage they are in. Knights will look to have fun with their children, but may not be reliable. Adventures keep calling them. A Prince is so focused on building something *for* the children that he doesn't have much energy left over to pay attention *to* them. No matter how much he loves them and wanted them, their mother will usually wish he would spend more time with them."

"And what's different about Kings?"

Claudia smiled. "Remember when we talked about computers and RAM? That RAM is how much you can have up on the screen at one time?"

Karen nodded. "You said almost all the RAM is used up by a Prince's career or work, making it hard for him to pay attention to anything else."

"Exactly. Well, when a man comes out of the Tunnel and becomes a King, much of the RAM is freed up. He doesn't need to focus on himself and his work like before. He naturally turns his focus toward what he cares about most. If he has children, he'll be able to pay attention to them in an entirely different way. If the children are older, this may come as a big surprise."

"In what way?" This was reminding Karen of something, but she couldn't quite put her finger on it.

"Children of Middle Princes may feel invisible to their fathers sometimes. He spends most of his time at work, and when he's home, he's preoccupied with something. Since the changes in a King are dramatic, they may wonder what inspired his new interest in them."

That's it! Karen distinctly remembered coming home from college and thinking a body snatcher had invaded her dad. He was different. She both loved it and didn't know how to handle it. Her dad wanted to know all about her life and he kept trying to do things for her.

She told Claudia what she remembered. "Is that because he had become a King?"

"Sounds like it. And if you had been a teenager, can you imagine? Probably would have driven you crazy. The real delight is a King with small children. They have much more attention to pay them. Often they are fascinated by their development and participate a lot more than they would have just a few years before. I am sure you have noticed the dads that come to parent conferences in the middle of the day. Aren't they mostly the silver haired dads instead of the younger ones?"

Karen thought about it. "Yes, I believe you're right."

Claudia smiled. "This is what I mean by there being advantages to having children with a King." She winked at her. "*Especially* with one who has waited *precisely* to spend more time with them."

Karen almost gasped. Wow. Double wow. Hmmm, maybe there's a *gold* lining.

"So Kings are the next topic, right? Is there anything I should do to get ready for Saturday?"

"I'll have to think about that." Claudia sat quietly with the pursed lips Karen had grown accustomed to. Burt must love that expression to have put it on the table, she thought.

"Besides talking about the stage of King," Claudia said, "we're going to talk about how to get ready for Mike being one. What he will need from you as a King is different than before and may challenge your relationships with all men."

Karen felt a little stab of fear. "What do you mean?"

Claudia looked serious. "Have you noticed how much women disparage men in our culture? They openly talk about them being 'pigs' or 'jerks' or say things like 'the world would be a better place if women were in charge'?"

How did Claudia know this? Karen wondered. She had to remember that Claudia was not an insulated little-old-lady-from-Pasadena type, even though she could pass for one.

"Now that you say that, yes, I can see it."

Claudia nodded. "Good. That makes it easier for me. What I want you to do between now and Saturday is notice how many men you respect and admire."

Again Karen was surprised; what an unusual assignment. "Okay, I'll do that. Anything else?"

"Yes," Claudia said, "keep listening. It's still one of the biggest keys to the kingdom."

Mike found the note Karen left with the two websites, as promised. While she was out, he logged onto the Internet and reviewed the two different programs. Interesting, he thought. The warrior thing appealed to him the most and, in a rare show of decisiveness, he registered for the San Diego weekend ten days away. There were classes in Los Angeles not long after, but he thought sooner was better and an entire weekend away appealed to him. He wondered how Karen would react; they didn't spend many weekends apart.

As he thought about it, he noticed he was doing the class as much for her as for himself. That surprised him. He wanted to do it for her. Why was that? he wondered. There was something about the way Karen was treating him lately that made him want to give her more. What was it? The only way he could put it was that he felt honored as a man. Claudia's philosophy and Karen's enthusiasm for it made him feel good. It made it fine for him to be who he was and to go through this Tunnel stuff.

Mike thought about his day. It had been normal in most respects: a site check, materials to follow up on, and the crew to confirm on another job. He had just as many questions and doubts as before, but now he didn't resist them. The questions even became interesting to him and sometimes he followed them along a trail that started to tell him something important about himself. As he made this site check, once again he was critical of the use of space and resources. He thought it was excessive. It made him dissatisfied with the end result of an otherwise perfectly good job. Now he noticed that being dissatisfied was different than before. He had certainly been dissatisfied many times in his life, but he just lived with it. Now he had a problem with being dissatisfied. Hmmm.

He remembered something else. All week he had been noticing the men on his crew. He could easily distinguish the Knights from the Princes. And there were two men who worked for him that clearly were not either of those. They were older than Mike and each accomplished in their trade. But now he was noticing them as people, instead of as craftsmen. He knew immediately that they were Kings. He recognized that, without thinking about it, he had always treated them with a different level of respect. Now he was noticing their physical presence. They were...solid. Like their bodies were made of a denser material than his.

Is that what's next for me? What will that be like? They seemed so...certain. Resolved. Then that same word again: *Solid*.

Sitting across from Claudia at the breakfast table, Burt noticed that she did not seem as excited about her session with Karen today as usual. Normally—at least normally for the last three weeks—she would be more exuberant in anticipation of her afternoon with her ever-more-promising student.

"Honey, you seem a little reticent about today. Is there something about this next stage that makes you nervous?" he asked, gently prodding her with this concern.

Claudia sighed. "This one is definitely going to be the most difficult. I knew the Tunnel would be hard on Karen, since Mike is in the Tunnel and she has a lot invested. But Kings...who they are and what they need will challenge everything she has been taught about men in her thirty-nine years of life."

"What has Karen been taught?"

"Actually, what all women have been taught…that's not precisely correct. It is more like what all women have 'learned.' I'm not sure anyone intentionally taught them all the rubbish they have come to accept."

Burt made a show of sitting up straighter. "Now you've got my attention! Rubbish? What rubbish?"

His enthusiasm brought a smile. Claudia said, "I appreciate you asking. Maybe if I talk this out with you, I'll be able to do a better job of teaching Karen today."

Burt could see she was about to embark on something, so he refilled his coffee and settled in to listen.

"Remember a few days ago when I told you that I have to clear away all the misconceptions Karen has in order to make a path for what I have to teach her? When we were talking about what makes this tiring?"

"Sure, but I didn't know exactly what you were referring to."

"To explain this, I'm going to have to go back a ways, back to where we started almost a month ago talking about the Covenant." Burt nodded his assent.

"During World War II, huge numbers of women went to work. Like never before in recent history. And they went to work making things that concerned survival—munitions, transportation, food. Whenever a person works in areas fundamental to survival itself, there is a sense of significance, there is an inherent *importance*."

"I think I see what you mean," Burt said. "Women took over jobs that men normally did. They had to, because most of us were at war. What they did was no longer an enhancement to what men provided. They became responsible for the most basic, necessary things."

Claudia was nodding. "Yes. And when anyone does that—when anyone provides what is critically needed, it gives that person a unique sense of himself or herself. To put it simply, women became heroes. We didn't get a ticker tape parade, but we felt it. And it happened to so many of us, that it forever altered our collective experience of being women. We found out how smart we are and how capable we are. We never wanted to go back to doing things that seemed unimportant."

Burt shook his head. "I see what you're saying, but I have to disagree. What women provide—what only women can provide, like beauty and comfort and nurturing—that's more than important. It's priceless."

Claudia grinned like he'd won a prize. "Exactly. I agree with you completely. But few women know this. We tasted 'important' and we were hooked. One way you could describe the last fifty years for women is the constant pursuit of the right to do everything that seems *important*. Whatever we think the important job is, we want the right to do it. And we have succeeded on most fronts. Women are doctors and lawyers and politicians and shuttle launch captains. We used to be secretaries to men in those positions."

She sighed. "But most of us don't know that we traded in 'priceless' for 'important.' We miss it, some more consciously than others, but we don't know how it happened. And we don't know how we damaged our relationships with men in the process."

"What happened?"

"This is just my theory, but I think it went something like this: Men came back after the war expecting things to go back to normal. In fact, being at war was devastating to them; they needed things to go back to normal, and quickly."

She paused and squeezed his hand. His own experience in the war had changed him forever. Claudia had been an extraordinary comfort for him.

She continued, "But having a taste of 'important,' women weren't willing to give it up. At least, enough women weren't willing. Women wanted those opportunities and it looked like men wouldn't give them to them. Women assumed it was because men thought we were too stupid or incapable. We were deeply hurt and insulted. I don't believe men thought these things. I believe women were trying to change an old institution—the workplace—overnight. And men were concerned with what they are always concerned with—having a job and then getting the job done. Since women didn't have a long track record of doing these jobs successfully, and they posed a threat to their jobs, men were skeptical. Combine that with men needing things to go back to normal, and there was a deadlock.

"This was when men became the *enemy*. And that's where the division between a woman's heart and a woman's mind began."

Burt was intrigued, as usual, by the twists and turns Claudia presented. "What do you mean?"

"Because women don't understand how powerful they are, diplomacy was not an option they considered. They went directly to fighting righteous battles. In order to put up a good fight, it works well to think your adversary is evil. Then you can go full throttle, no holds barred. You can hate your enemy and hate can fuel many confrontations."

She paused. "But in our hearts, we naturally love men. Just as men naturally love women. This made it hard to hate men. Therefore, we picked another arena—instead of the heart, that of the mind. We started changing how we think of men in ways that would fuel the battle. We needed to invalidate men and validate women. We needed to think that women are better than men. It's a natural response to the insult we felt, too. Since we felt insulted by men, we needed to degrade them to make their insults sting less. If someone you respect insults you, it hurts. If you are insulted by someone you think is a jerk, you just move on. Mind me, I don't think anyone did all of this consciously. It just happened, like dominoes falling."

Claudia sipped her tea. "Combine the perceived insults with some very real wrongs perpetrated by some men, add the women's 'gab factor,' and this new perception of men traveled fast. 'Men are male-chauvinist pigs' got into women's thinking quickly. Over the years, it became shortened to the simpler 'men are pigs.'"

Burt could see what she was talking about, except, "What do you mean by the 'gab factor'?"

"How much women talk, naturally." Claudia smiled, clearly amused with herself.

"Let me see if I've got this right," Burt responded. "You're saying that during the war, women experienced being important. Essentially, what men experience. They liked it and they didn't want to give it up. Which put them in a fight against men, because we weren't prepared for everything that meant. And they were insulted; because women thought that we thought you all were stupid or something. Then, because they couldn't hate us, in order to fight us better, and to make the insult hurt less, women starting thinking men were jerks. Is that the gist of it?"

Claudia laughed. "I knew if I talked this out with you, it would become clearer! I like how you put it." She smiled at him. "Yes, that is 'the gist' of it. We became incredibly critical of everything men do and how they do it. Because we have got to prove that we can do it better. There is even a song to that effect."

Burt shook his head. "Amazing. Does it matter at all that some of the assumptions are incorrect?"

Claudia laughed again. "Only if you are concerned with reality, dear. But by now, the idea that men are terrible is entrenched. It is difficult to break it loose, even with facts."

Burt was shaking his head again. "Truly amazing. No wonder they call it the war between the sexes. Complete with misinformation campaigns."

Claudia chuckled and then grew serious. "The sad part is how much suffering for both men and women has come out of this. Don't get me wrong; I am not saying women should not have fought, or shouldn't keep fighting for the right to do all the important things. Although I would have preferred diplomacy, the results have been unprecedented. Imagine, women not needing men to provide for them and protect them in order to survive. Finally, equal partnerships are possible. It's terribly exciting."

Burt was skeptical. "I know women think equality is a good thing, but from my point of view, that is a step down for women. Why would you want to be merely important when you are already priceless? What women provide, men couldn't do in a thousand years. Just think about who has been dying for whom all this time. It is men dying to protect women. That should tell women who *we* think matters."

Claudia smiled. "I know, honey. Men know who women are and how much power we wield. It's women who are in the dark. They think they are walking around unarmed and they have picked up grenades and machetes. Sadly, they don't hesitate to use them."

"What do you mean, exactly?"

"Well, because we think men are our adversaries, we treat men that way. You never want an adversary to be stronger than you. Therefore, women do things to weaken men, to steal some of their power. Little things that bleed men slowly, like criticizing and complaining. Or more quickly, like withdrawing from you altogether with the silent treatment or taking you apart when you're late. Or like a cancer, by never having anything you do be good enough." Claudia shook her head sadly. "If only women knew that these things were unnecessary."

Burt saw a chance and took it. "I've been wanting to talk to you about that."

"About what?" Claudia looked surprised.

"About women knowing what you know."

He held up his hand when she started to protest. "Let me finish." Claudia sat back. "I think you have shown already that what you know is important to other people. Didn't you tell me Mike is doing better just by finding out he's in the Tunnel? And look at Karen—isn't her life better?"

Claudia nodded but wouldn't look up at him. "Claudia, sweetheart. I know how much you *need* to teach other people. Just look at your hands. Do you remember what they were like a month ago? When was the last time they hurt you?"

Claudia opened her hands in front of her. She stretched her fingers out farther than she had in years. Then she looked up at him and smiled. "This would be easier for you if you were still a King, wouldn't it? Then you could just give me the advice you think I need." Her eyes twinkled, teasing him.

Burt chuckled. "Yes, it's true. I would just come right out and tell you what to do. Being an Elder certainly has its drawbacks."

"Okay, honey. What is the question I should be asking that you would love to answer?" She smiled at him, with what he hoped was compassion.

"You could ask me for advice on how you might contribute what you know about men and women to many, many people."

Claudia looked at him, her eyes suddenly tearing up. "I'm not ready yet." She wiped a tear that had escaped down her cheek. "I know you suggested I find someone like Karen, and that same day, I did. You were right; she exists, and better than I hoped. But this process has been difficult, for me and for Karen. For my own conscience, I have to finish this and make sure it turns out right, before I can think of any-body else."

Burt understood. He had more faith in her than she did in herself. Just as she always had more faith in him. That was as is should be. He picked up her hand and brought it to his lips. "Whenever you're ready, I'll be here."

For the first time, Karen felt reluctant about her session with Claudia. Usually the morning passed too slowly while she waited in anticipation of more mind-blowing information. Today, she was sure she had completely failed the assignment Claudia had given her. Karen hoped she wouldn't ask about it.

When they were situated at the extraordinary table once again, with their hot chocolate and lap blankets, Claudia asked, "So, how did you do with your preparation? How many men did you see that you respect and admire?"

Karen couldn't suppress a groan. She took a couple of sips of cocoa to stall. "Actually, Claudia, not a single one. I am embarrassed to say it. Mike comes the closest, but I got stuck on 'admire.' That's a big one. I find it hard to admire any man."

To her surprise Claudia smiled. "You're smiling?" Karen asked. "I thought for sure I had blown it."

Claudia reached over and patted her hand. If the difficulty of a session could be measured in how many times Claudia patted her hand, then this one was starting off at a run. "Don't worry, dear, it's not your fault."

"It's not?"

Claudia shook her head. "No, it's not. Can you think of any woman you know who respects many men?"

Karen thought about it. "You obviously respect Burt, but that wouldn't count, would it?" Claudia chuckled and shook her head no.

Karen thought some more. "Then I can't think of any. I know women who admire celebrities, but they don't know them. If they did, I doubt they would respect them. It's hard to respect men—they screw up so much of the time."

Now Claudia was grinning at her. "Perfect. Thank you!"

"What? That they screw up? Like giving you advice when you need them to sympathize? Or how they never know what you want, no matter how many hints you leave?"

Claudia shook her head but smiled again. "Honestly, Karen, I have been trying to figure out how to teach you about Kings, and I wasn't sure how to do it. But you have shown me the way."

"I have?"

"Yes, you have. Tell me, how do you know they 'screw up,' as you say, all the time?"

Without hesitation, Karen said, "Because they don't do what they should have done."

"And how do you know they don't do what they should have done?"

Karen caught on, and laughed. "Because they don't do what I would have done!"

Claudia nodded. "Right, they don't do what you would have done. But it goes beyond that, doesn't it? Isn't it what all women would have done? Isn't it what we think all women know is the *right* thing to do?"

Karen considered this. She thought about the many sessions with her friends evaluating what someone's husband or boyfriend had done versus what he "should" have done. They almost always agreed on the basics of what should have been. "Yes, I think so. But isn't that because women in general are smarter than men and more mature?"

She couldn't believe it; Claudia was actually cracking up! She was slapping her thigh, laughing, and shaking her head.

"What? What did I say?" Karen asked.

Claudia shook her head some more. "It's not what you said. It's what made it possible to say it. And even more so, to think it. It just amazes me."

Karen felt uncomfortable. She didn't like not getting the joke. Was Claudia laughing at her?

As if reading her mind—again—Claudia said, "Karen, I'm not laughing at you. I am laughing at us—at women. We are certain that our way is the best way, and we can't even consider anything else. We can't even see anything else. And, especially, we can't even see men."

"What do you mean, we can't *see* men?"

Karen waited while Claudia calmed herself down. "Remember before we started talking about the Stages of Development, how what Mike had done in his twenties and thirties didn't make sense to you? Without understanding the stages, Knights seem immature about fun and adventure, and Princes seem stubbornly, selfishly obsessed with their work. By learning about the stages, you can now *see* men go through them. You can *see* Mike being in the Tunnel. And just by being able to see it, you are able to respond better."

"Are you saying that there is more we can't see about men? More than just the stages?"

"Oh, dear Lord, yes."

"Like what?" Karen asked hopefully.

Claudia took a sip of her cocoa and shook her head. "I don't know how long it would take to tell you all of it. Maybe years. Just about everything that men do and all the ways that men are, we assume to be immature or selfish or inconsiderate or underdeveloped. Usually some version of acting up and misbehaving. We hardly *see* men at all. And we rarely see the real reason men have for their behavior."

"Could you at least give me an example?" Karen practically begged. She waited, letting Claudia think, and hoping her patience would be rewarded.

Finally Claudia said, "I'll name a few and then I'll show you two things that are *not* what they seem."

Karen positioned her pen over her paper, ready to capture every morsel.

Claudia began, "These are some of the things that women misinterpret: we think men being competitive all the time is immature. We think they are lousy listeners and that's because they are inconsiderate. We think men are 'emotionally unavailable' or 'cut off from their emotions' because they are undeveloped in some fundamental way. And we think men put their needs first because they are self-centered or selfish or inconsiderate, or all three," she concluded. "Just to name a few."

As Claudia went through her list, Karen couldn't help but nod in agreement. She definitely thought all those things. Wasn't it true?

"And you are saying that we think that because we can't *see* men?"

Claudia nodded. "Absolutely. And because we can't see them, we don't respect them and we are unable to admire them. And that makes us totally unequipped to relate to a King."

Ahh, Karen thought. Kings. Yes, today is about Kings. That's where this is going. "I really want to know about Kings," she said, "but this business of *seeing men* is fascinating to me. You said you would show me two things that are not what they seem?"

Claudia nodded again. "Yes. The first one you figured out on your own, which is why I invited you to become my student. Remember the first night at the coffee house when you told me what you noticed about Mike needing time to adjust when he comes home?"

Karen remembered well. "That seemed important to you at the time, but I couldn't guess why."

Now Claudia smiled. "I think you watch me as carefully as I watch you," she raised her eyebrows, seeking confirmation.

Karen smiled back. "Like you, I am a teacher. You have to see the subtle clues that show you are getting through. Do it for almost fifteen years and it makes a person sensitive. At least, if you are committed to being a great teacher."

Claudia looked happy for a moment. She seemed to relax in some way too, like some issue was being resolved. Karen knew better than to ask. She hoped someday Claudia would tell her what it was all about.

Claudia picked up where she had digressed. "What you noticed about Mike is what we call 'Transition Time.' When men come home from work, or change from any type of activity to another, they need a period of adjustment. Women, paying attention to many things at once, usually don't need this. Being unable to *see* men, few women recognize this need. Mostly, women just think that the sort of far off look on his face and detached way of moving through the house is because he's not happy to be home or he doesn't care about them. It is nothing of the sort. It's just his Transition Time."

Karen couldn't suppress a grin. Finally, something she had been doing right! "You call it Transition Time? When he's adjusting to being at home? Then me leaving him alone is the best thing to do?"

Claudia nodded. "And the other things you do, too. You stop what you are doing to greet him, welcoming him home. And you recognize when the transition is over and he's ready to be with you, and make yourself available. That is the part that women who don't know about Transition Time find impossible. Since their feelings are hurt by how he is at first, when he finally comes to them, they are angry or cold. That makes him feel pushed away. It's one of the ways that women prevent the intimacy they crave."

Karen smiled. "It's great to find out I don't do everything wrong."

Claudia slowly rubbed her hands together. Karen noticed that her fingers didn't seem as gnarled as before—or was that just her imagination?

Claudia said, "What you have been doing wrong is not your fault. With little useful information available, and a point of view that prevents us from seeing men in the first place, women are bound to fail with men. No matter how intelligent they are."

Karen considered this. Maybe all the misery she and her friends shared was unnecessary? "And there is something besides Transition Time that is not what it seems?"

"Let's take something else along those same lines," Claudia continued. "Throughout the stages, I have talked about men changing their focus. As Pages and Knights they're focused on adventure, as Princes, they're focused on building. In the Tunnel, they're focused on all the questions plaguing them. Do you remember me using the word 'focus' often?"

Karen nodded. At the time, she had thought it was just Claudia's quaint way of speaking.

"I use the word focus because it has everything to do with being a man. It is what men do naturally—they focus. And they focus on one thing at a time. It's the way they are designed to think. You might have even heard them say something about it. Like when we're going in five different directions, they say, 'Slow down, let's take this one thing at a time.'"

Karen could immediately remember both her dad and Mike saying that.

Claudia continued, "Men are what we call Single Focused. It is a remarkable quality. It is one of the things that make them able to remember details, like all the statistics of a ball game or an entire sports season. They are utterly focused on that one thing when they are participating in it. Can you see that?"

Karen was seeing it: Mike reading the newspaper. Her dad fixing the car. Casey tacking up the collages. There was an intensity about each of them.

"Wow, I do see it. But I've never noticed it before. At least not like a different way of thinking. They just seem…limited. That's what you're talking about, isn't it? They are not what they seem?"

Claudia smiled again. "Exactly. Because women are not Single Focused—although they can be for short periods of time—we normally don't recognize it as valid behavior. Some women even think it means men are stupid. This is what has us think men are lousy listeners. Because we talk to them during Transition Time, when they are focused on transitioning, or when they are focused on something else. Have you ever had two people talking to you at once?"

"Of course. In my classroom practically every day."

"And you can only listen to one at a time right?" Karen nodded. "That is exactly what it's like for men. If they are reading the newspaper, or getting dressed for work, they can't listen to us, too."

"So are you saying that we think men are lousy listeners because of *when* we talk to them?"

Claudia nodded. "Men are actually great listeners. Because, when it's *time* to listen, that is what they are focused on. Women rarely focus on just listening to another person. You've been practicing lately; I'll bet you can see the difference."

That's for sure, Karen thought. She had changed her marriage just by listening. And, she realized, also by *seeing*. The Stages of Development had made it possible for her to see Mike's behavior and make sense of it. Instead of being ridiculous or frustrating, it had become understandable. Wow.

But then she thought of some times when Mike really was a lousy listener. "Claudia, there have been times when I was talking to Mike and he wouldn't listen to me at all. He kept interrupting me with his opinion."

"Were you discussing something?" Claudia asked.

"I think so. Like recently, we were discussing last week's election results. I voted for a bond issue for education and he voted against it. But I could hardly get a word in edgewise. I thought that was lousy listening."

Claudia nodded. "That's understandable. But again, if you see it for what it was, you might change your mind."

"So what was it?"

"Did you ask Mike for some time to tell him what you thought about the bond issue?"

"No, I was reading the paper and we just started talking about it."

Claudia nodded again. "See, it's because it wasn't 'listen' time. It was 'discuss the issues' time. Men will out-defend their opinions over a woman's every time. They have to. And if they can't, they'll walk away."

"Why is that?"

"That's a whole other topic. Again, something that seems one way but is not. Maybe another time. But let's go back to the listening thing. When you told Mike about Princes and the Tunnel, how did you set it up?"

"I asked for time to tell him what I had learned from you."

"And what happened?"

Karen smiled as she remembered it vividly. "Exactly that. He just listened and listened until I was done. No matter how long it took...*Amazing*."

Claudia just looked at her, with her head cocked to the side. "Are you starting to *see* them?"

Karen nodded over and over again. "Yep. And the more I see, the more I *want* to see. But it makes me feel like I've been blind." She paused, considering if this was the right time. "Claudia?"

"Yes, dear?"

"Ever since you started teaching me about men, I've wanted to teach other women. I don't want them to suffer as I have; I want them to see men, too."

Claudia was squinting. Karen wasn't sure what that meant and she continued, "Have you thought about teaching anyone else?"

Still squinting, Claudia said quietly, "I've thought about it," her body visibly stiffening.

Ignoring her own observations, Karen decided to go for it. "Would you consider letting me teach other women?" She rushed on, "I would only tell them what you wanted me to. Or we could do it together. I have all my notes from every session. I've even typed them into my computer and organized them like a curriculum." She stopped, afraid she had said too much.

To Karen's dismay, Claudia looked like she was suffering terribly. The soft pink had left her cheeks and she instantly looked much older. She suddenly excused herself and walked quickly inside the house.

Karen was devastated. *What have I done? How did I hurt her?* Then she thought of herself and Mike. *Oh, no, what if she won't teach me anymore? I don't understand Kings!*

Miserable, she waited for Claudia's return. Not knowing what else to do, she traced the carvings on the table with her finger. She could understand why Burt adored his wife. *She is an extraordinary woman,* she thought. *Oh God, please don't let me have ruined this.*

Burt had been looking out the window, checking the angle of the sun, when Claudia rushed into the house. He guessed at the reason for Claudia's distress and thought it might partly be his fault, for pushing her this morning to teach others. The last time he had seen her look that upset was when Myra, for the final time, refused her inheritance. To a lesser degree, it was the same expression he had seen on Claudia's face just a few short weeks ago, when she returned from the doctor's office. He did not want to go back to that. With this much at stake, he had to do something.

He watched Karen for a moment and decided she was probably the more miserable of the two. He wiped his hands on his coveralls and went out to the garden. Karen looked up in surprise as he took Claudia's seat. He could see tears wetting her cheeks, so he took out his handkerchief and offered it to her.

"It's clean," he said.

Karen accepted the hanky and wiped her face. She looked up at him tentatively and when he nodded, she went ahead and delicately blew her nose.

After she collected herself, she said, "I didn't mean to upset her, Burt, honestly. I just asked if we could teach other women what she has taught me. I would never hurt her on purpose…She's changed my life." With that fresh tears started down her face.

Burt waited and studied Karen's face. Really quite lovely, he thought. Her golden brown eyes were a shade darker than her caramel skin. The fringe of black lashes set them off nicely. He was sorry to see the suffering they revealed.

"It's not your fault, Karen. This has upset Claudia for many years. It is the only place in her life that she suffers. I just recently understood it all myself. It was a big step for her, taking you as a student. It was against a promise she made to her family a long time ago."

"A promise?"

"Her family created an agreement among themselves. They promised to only teach their own family members in order that the information wouldn't be used to hurt anyone."

"Hurt anyone? How could it hurt anyone? This information *helps* people. It has already helped me and Mike."

Burt said patiently, "You have a good heart, Karen. Claudia saw that right off and she was correct. But even you, if backed into a corner, might use what you've learned to lash out at a man. According to Claudia, plenty of women feel backed into a corner most of the time."

Karen looked perplexed, but sufficiently calmed down. Burt got to his feet. "I'm sure she'll be back out soon. Can I get you something? Some tea perhaps? Or some tomato soup?"

Karen smiled at him and he thought again, how lovely. "No thank you, Burt. I'll just wait."

"Don't fret," Burt said as he knocked his knuckles on the tabletop. "She made a promise to her family, but she'll work this out between her and her boss. I'm sure it'll turn out just fine."

Karen's brows knit together. "Her boss?"

Burt raised his eyebrows and pointed with a long knobby finger up at the clouds. "Her boss."

Claudia wiped her face with a hand towel, patted the color back into her cheeks and left her bathroom. She was at peace again. She started back out to the garden but saw Burt sitting at the table with Karen. What is he up to? she wondered. She stood at the French doors and kept watching until she saw him get up. When he pointed up at the clouds, she concluded he must have been talking about the weather. Making polite conversation, covering for her, she thought gratefully.

She crossed paths with Burt and he smiled sweetly at her. "Can I get you some tea, honey?" he asked a little *too* sweetly.

She shook her head, "No, thank you." As he made his way back to his shop, she heard him whistling *I'm Popeye The Sailor Man* and wondered again, what's he up to?

She sat across from Karen and instantly recognized Burt's handkerchief sitting on the table. That drew her attention to Karen's eyes, which were slightly reddened.

She said, "Karen, I am sorry I got upset. It wasn't you. The offer you made was generous, and in different circumstances, might be perfect. Give me a chance to think about it, okay?"

Karen nodded. "Sure. Take all the time you need. I'm very sorry. I hope you know I would never hurt you intentionally."

Claudia nodded. "I do know, dear. I do. Don't worry about it, okay? What do you say we do what we came here for? Are you ready to learn about Kings?"

Karen looked relieved and quickly picked up her pen again. Claudia remembered that somewhere Karen's other notes were neatly typed into a computer. She wasn't sure how she felt about that. She was sure the typing of them had helped Karen to retain a lot, and that was a good thing. But was the information safe there? Safer than in your feeble old brain, she thought, with uncharacteristic bitterness. Computers don't die, right?

Calming herself, Claudia took a deep breath, and began, "What we have already talked about, about *seeing* men, should help with learning about this stage. Imagine, if you will, a process of becoming, of building, of creating, that lasts years and years. Over those years, a man becomes more sure of himself, more certain."

She paused. "Then comes an introspective period, where everything is questioned, including who he is. That period ends with a man defining himself. Not from who he has been, not from what his parents taught him, nor what his friends think, nor from what his family wants or who his wife needs him to be. Just standing on his own, he says who he is. Bravely. Perhaps concerned about the consequences, but facing them nevertheless."

She concluded, "This is a King."

Claudia watched Karen absorb that. She assumed she was thinking of Mike and what was soon to come. Claudia could see a mixture of dread and hope on her face. Then Karen's face brightened.

"Yes?" Claudia asked.

"Sorry to interrupt, but you reminded me of something. Do you ever watch movies?"

Claudia nodded. "Quite often, actually. They are great for research."

"Really? How so?"

"Depending on whether they were made by a man or a woman, they reveal many things. Movies made by men reflect their values and can also show what men take for granted. It reveals what is real for them, what they rarely question the validity of. Movies made by women have helped me to see what has happened in our culture. They often express the level of anger and resentment women feel."

Karen looked liked she wanted to ask about that, but went on, "The reason I brought it up is that last weekend Mike and I rented *American Beauty*. Have you seen it?"

She nodded. "Yes, I have. What did you think of it?"

"Well, the part I was fascinated by is the Kevin Spacey character. Did I get this right? Is he in the Tunnel in the beginning and then he comes out and acts much stronger?"

Claudia nodded again. "Very good. I believe that's what's happening. But I don't know if the screenwriter meant it that way."

Claudia continued, "When a man becomes a King, he is a 100% finished man. He is turned out. Grown up, if you will. I like to say, 'This cake is baked.' You can't change him, you can't modify him, you can't add on any after-market features. You might be able to frost him."

Claudia smiled at her own mixed metaphors; this could be fun. She continued, "When a man comes out of the Tunnel, he has decided who he is and everything related to that. He probably won't be aware of it all consciously, but scratch the surface and you will find it. He knows who he is and who he is not. He knows what he is interested in and what he considers a waste of his time. He knows what he wants to provide and for whom. Again, he may not think all these things consciously, but when faced with a situation, his position will be certain."

Karen was scribbling furiously, and Claudia slowed up. If this is going to become something for other women, we might need a complete set of notes, she thought spontaneously. Where did that thought come from? she wondered nervously.

Karen looked up and Claudia took it as a sign to continue. "When men become Kings, they gain new capacities and their needs change. Like I said before, they don't have to pay attention to themselves as much. Having this attention available for other people often has them like to teach and makes them natural mentors. This is part of what they are able to provide."

She added, "Kings have a huge capacity for giving and providing. But there is a catch."

"A catch?"

"A King has specific ideas about what he wants to provide. On the one hand, if you need it, and appreciate it, he can overwhelm you with his generosity. On the other hand, if you need something that he is not interested in providing, he will tell you to go elsewhere. As one King put it, 'Don't ask us for what we don't have to give. Ask for what we do have, and we'll give you all we can.'"

Karen was nodding and writing. Claudia waited.

"Did you notice how I said 'not interested in providing'?" Claudia asked.

Karen nodded. "I did, but I just assumed that was your way of speaking again."

Claudia shook her head. "I speak precisely, especially when I am talking about men. Some of what you call 'my way of speaking' would more likely be because I duplicate the way men actually speak, or speak about themselves.

"'Focus' is a word men use a lot. And 'interested' is a word Kings use a lot. It is one of the ways you can recognize Kings, by their use of the word 'interested.' More specifically, by the phrase, 'I'm not interested in that.' They will say it quietly, which may make a woman think she can change his mind; but she can't. Kings will not do what they are not 'interested in.' In fact, I have seen men leave lucrative, prestigious positions because they were being compelled to do something they were not interested in. Can you remember a man saying something like 'I'm not interested in that'?"

Claudia waited while Karen thought about it. Suddenly she said, "Yes! When Mike and I went back to Chicago for Christmas last year, my mother was trying to get my dad to go to a performance of the Nutcracker with her. My dad said, 'I'm not interested in that. You should go with someone else.' Is that what you mean?"

"Exactly. And did your mother try to persuade him?"

"Oh, absolutely, she worked on him for three days. But he never changed his mind. I thought he was being stubborn and inconsiderate of her feelings."

Claudia was shaking her head. "Once again, it's not what it seems. Your dad was not being stubborn and inconsiderate—like something he would do on purpose. Your dad was just being a King. Kings can't do what they are not interested in. It is against their nature. It betrays their sense of self, which is something they can't do without a tremendous amount of suffering."

"I thought it would be much easier for my dad to just give in and accommodate her. You're saying it would have been harder?"

"Yes, much harder. Throughout their lives, men do a lot of accommodating. They have to, because women and children and customers and employers can be demanding. But after a man becomes a King, accommodation is not something he can easily do. Their sense of self has become complete, has become solid, and therefore not easily betrayed."

Claudia waited and watched Karen's face. She could see the connections being made and she began to feel better.

Karen said, "When we started a few weeks ago, you told me that the Stages of Development have to do with a man's sense of self. That he is literally building his self. Can you say more about that?"

Claudia welcomed the question and was, again, impressed by her student. "You could say that the Stages of Development are the stages of the development of a man's self, a man's identity. But it is paradoxical. On the one hand, with each stage he becomes more himself. On the other hand, who he is was already there, and at each stage he has to keep truing himself up."

"More, please?" Karen asked, looking hopeful.

Claudia nodded. "As a Knight, he knows that how he is going to grow is by being *out there*. This is why it is difficult for teenage boys to hang around the house. They know instinctively that they aren't learning anything about *life*. But being out in the world, he can't just conform. Even though there is enormous pressure to conform, he's got to be true to himself. And boys will admire other boys who are true to themselves. 'Sellout' is a huge insult for any generation.

"Then, as early Princes, they have to find a career that fits who they are. It's got to feel right. If it doesn't, he'll have to come to terms with that later."

"What do you mean?" Karen asked.

Claudia elaborated, glad for the chance to clarify this point that she hadn't made with Karen the previous week. "If an early Prince is forced into a type of work by his situation, then later on he'll have to reconcile it. For example, let's take a young man who is artistic in some way, let's say, a musician. Because he has a family to support, he gets a steady job in a shoe store. For this generation, it's probably a computer store, but let's just say it's a shoe store. Being a hard worker, over the years he gets promoted. Step-by-step he becomes the store manager and then maybe a regional manager. But it never fits him. This is where accommodating comes in. During his Prince years, he keeps accommodating his family's needs, his employer's needs, and so on. Then he enters the Tunnel. That's where it becomes intolerable. This is where your Kevin Spacey character in *American Beauty* quit his job. Because in the Tunnel he realizes that he is about to become *forever* the shoe man, or the advertising man, or whatever. But it never fit and it still doesn't. Only now, it's intolerable. This is why you have forty-year-olds starting bands, or returning to their art and sculpture, or inventions, or whatever their passion was before they had to make a living."

Karen looked concerned. "So what happens to them? Do they stay in the Tunnel like that?"

Claudia thought a moment. "It seems that they either pick a new area to build in and go back to being a middle Prince, or they just give in and reluctantly continue whatever they were doing. The first choice will take courage and determination and cost them time and probably money. The second choice will cost them part of their dignity and a lot of their power."

Karen was shaking her head. "What would have a man continue doing what he doesn't want to do? Why would he pick that?"

Claudia responded, "Lots of reasons, Karen. Men are sensitive about their obligations. He may choose to fulfill other people's expectations of him—expectations he has accepted—rather than do what he wants to do. It is another way of being honorable. Never underestimate the importance of being honorable to a man. Or he may lack the support of a woman he loves—a woman he needs—and not be willing to risk losing her. He'd rather lose a part of himself than lose her."

Now Karen was shaking her head. "Men are a lot more complicated than I thought."

Claudia chuckled. "Never say that to a man, okay? Men think they are simple creatures. They are, in fact, direct creatures, but not simple. They don't realize how many paradoxes they reconcile every day."

Karen kept writing. Then she asked, changing the subject, "How else can you tell that a man is a King? Besides him saying the word 'interested'?"

While Claudia would have enjoyed a side trip into the many paradoxes of men, she thought Karen wise to get back to Kings. "Just to be clear, what you'll hear most is the phrase, 'I'm *not* interested.' What he is interested in, he'll do without much fanfare. And you'd have a hard time stopping him. Besides that, the best way to recognize a King is by his body, by his stature. Men in different stages appear differently. Knights actually look full of themselves, because they are and should be. Princes lose that confidence and their bodies become less visible. They seem more compact, but also like you could push your hand through their bodies. Late Princes walk taller, with more substance, but it's not the same as a King. When a King enters a room you get the sense that he commands whatever space he is taking up. He looks very 'solid,' as though if you pushed on him, he wouldn't budge at all. Kings have stature. And it doesn't matter how tall or big they are. It doesn't even matter how big their kingdom is."

"What do you mean?"

"It would be easy to automatically assume that Kings are 'successful' in the normal use of the term. Being a King has nothing to do with material success. A King is a man who knows who he is, period. Like Popeye saying, 'I yam what I yam.' No matter the wealth or size of his kingdom, a man is still a King; and other men will recognize that."

Claudia chuckled. "Of course, there are Kings who aspire to be Emperors, but that's an ambition issue, not a stage of development."

Karen finished writing. "What else can you tell me about Kings?"

"Well, this brings in another subject, but do you remember earlier when I said that a man will out-argue a woman's opinions every time? And if he can't, he'll walk away?"

Karen nodded. "When we were talking about men being good listeners or lousy listeners."

"Exactly. Men and women have very different relationships to their opinions. For a woman, her opinion can include what she thinks about a particular topic at the moment. She doesn't even have to know a lot about the subject to have an opinion. For example, I could ask a woman, 'What do you think about the United Nations?' and a woman would tell me what she thinks, whether she knows a little or a lot on that subject. For a man, his opinion is a much more serious matter. You have probably heard a man respond to a question with, 'I don't know enough about that to have an opinion.' That surprises women. A woman may even think, 'What? Is he stupid?'

"But he's not stupid. He just regards his opinions differently. He develops his opinions from a combination of the information he has gathered and his values. He needs to have sufficient information. And his values are part of the definition of himself. This is why men will defend their opinions vigorously. Because they are defending an expression of themselves."

"Wow. I never saw that before. I just thought they were pigheaded and would sacrifice anything to win an argument!"

Claudia laughed. "Yes, it could seem that way. When you can't *see* a man…well, you already know what I would say." Karen nodded in agreement and smiled.

Claudia continued, "When a man becomes a King, his sense of self becomes extremely strong. Plus, he is older and therefore has had more time to gather information. Therefore, what you have in a King is someone with plenty of opinions. Furthermore, since Kings are the kings of providing, one of the things they will often provide is their opinion. And what a King needs is for his opinions to be respected. To disrespect his opinions is the same as disrespecting him. And this is the crux of the problem. Kings need respect and admiration like they need food and water. And as we have seen before, women are ill-equipped to provide respect and admiration since they see men, as you put it earlier, as 'screwing up all the time.'"

"So when I think a man is being pigheaded and a jerk for advocating his opinion, you're saying he's trying to provide something for me? Yikes! Do I have to just agree with him no matter what I think?" Karen looked horrified.

Claudia laughed and shook her head. "Treating his opinion with respect does not mean you have to agree. Just don't *disrespect* it. He is offering a gift. As the receiver, you get to accept or decline. But it would be good to do either graciously."

Again Claudia waited while Karen wrote. This sure goes slower this way, she thought. Then, why am I doing it? she asked herself. Just in case…just in case, what, Missy? To quiet the conversation in her mind, she kept going.

"This brings up another issue women often have with Kings. Besides needing to be respected and admired, Kings need what they have to give to be well received. They have a tremendous amount to give and they need someone who will accept it and appreciate it. Unfortunately, few women are good at receiving. In fact, most are terrible at it."

That got Karen's attention. "You mean like when my dad became a King and kept wanting to do stuff for me?" Claudia nodded. Karen continued, "It was hard to let him. I thought he was offering because he thought I couldn't do it myself. I needed to prove to him that I could."

Claudia nodded again. "Ah, yes. That is one of the biggest barriers to receiving. Thinking you have to prove you can do it yourself. Confusing thing is…who are you proving it to?"

"To my dad, of course."

"Really? What if I told you that your dad already knew you could do it?"

"Then why did he offer to do it?"

"Because he *wanted* to *provide* that for you."

"How do you know that?"

Claudia chuckled. This was one of her favorite things about men. The difference between the way women thought and the way men thought just amazed her.

"How I know is because he offered. When men offer, they mean it. We don't believe it because sometimes women offer to get *credit for offering,* when we are secretly hoping it *won't* be accepted. Men offer and are hoping it *will* be accepted."

Claudia could see that this was almost too much for Karen. She sat back in her chair and kept shaking her head. "If what you say is true, I have dashed the hopes of many men. Especially those of some very young men."

Claudia nodded. "Of course. Can you imagine if Santa Claus showed up with gifts and children turned him away? Men are extremely generous and giving by nature. It's no accident Santa Claus is a man."

Karen laughed. "You say that as if you believe in Santa Claus."

"Of course I do," Claudia said, quite seriously.

Karen looked doubtful, but she clearly had more pressing concerns. "So this 'receiving' business—to get along with a King, it's something you have to be good at?"

Claudia nodded. "Absolutely. If you won't accept and appreciate his gifts, he will have to find someone who will."

Karen looked stricken. Good, Claudia thought. It's that serious.

"How…how do I…how do I get better at it?"

"How do you expand your ability to receive?" Claudia clarified.

"Yes, I guess that is what I'm asking."

Claudia shook her head. "Receiving is an essential key to the kingdom. But to tell you everything about it would require days and days. Because it would involve many more topics than the Stages of Development. And I have already brought in too much information beyond the stages."

"Can you at least get me started?" Karen begged.

Claudia was sympathetic. Receiving was such a difficult thing for women to do these days.

"Okay. I'll point you in the right direction. The first couple of things you have already started to see. Watch when you are trying to prove something to a man. That will get in the way of receiving. Next, assume if he offers, he means it. He wants to give that. Third, b-r-e-a-t-h-e, breathe. Breathe deeply. Breathing is a physical act of receiving. It will help you do it mentally and emotionally as well. And, last but not least, receiving is all about noticing."

"Noticing?"

"Yes. Noticing. Paying attention to what is happening. Paying attention to what is being given and why. Take a rest from the other nine things you are doing as a normal multitasking woman and stop and notice the gifts. Pause for them; brake for them; give them your attention. And notice out loud. Say what you are seeing, say what you admire or are tickled by. Say what makes you happy."

Karen looked overwhelmed—she wasn't even writing. Tears rolled down her cheeks. She wiped her face with Burt's handkerchief, then blew her nose and looked up at Claudia, miserably.

"Mike has given me so much. I hardly ever stop to notice. And when I do, I'm too embarrassed to say anything."

Claudia nodded sympathetically. "Yes, authentically receiving a gift can make a person vulnerable. It is literally opening yourself up and letting the gift inside. That is why it is special."

Karen wiped her eyes again. "Casey brought me a gift yesterday. He saved his potato chips from his lunch, and he gave them to me."

"And what did you do?"

She shook her head. "I told him I couldn't take them from him, that I know they are his favorite."

"And how did Casey react? Did he look happy or relieved that you wouldn't accept them?"

Karen shook her head again. "No, he didn't look happy at all; he looked bummed."

Claudia nodded. "Casey is a very young man, and he hasn't yet learned to cover his feelings well. He showed you what all men feel when we won't accept their gifts."

Karen looked sad. Claudia made a decision. "Karen, I think we have had enough for today. If I think of anything else you need to know about Kings, I'll tell you Wednesday night. Are we still meeting after yoga, even though Thanksgiving is the next day?"

Karen nodded. "I hope so. It helps me a lot, and I enjoy it."

"Great. Me too. Karen?"

"Yes?"

"Burt and I were wondering if you and Mike will be in town next weekend. We would like to invite you to have Thanksgiving with us."

Karen looked pleased; then her expression changed. "I forgot to tell you that Mike signed up for that New Warrior class. He's going to San Diego next weekend."

"Really? Well, that's perfect. That will give you some time to get ready for him."

"What do you mean? I was kind of bummed to be at home by myself on Thanksgiving weekend."

"We'll talk about it Wednesday night. I have filled your head enough. But having time to yourself will be perfect. Is the class four days? Will Mike go down on Thursday?"

Karen shook her head. "Oh, no. He doesn't drive down until Friday. It goes from Friday until Sunday night. I would love to have Thanksgiving dinner with you, but I need to ask Mike. Who all will be here? Are your children coming?"

Claudia shook her head. "No, Max is in Oregon. He and his wife will come down with the boys for Christmas. And it's just not Myra's thing, spending time with the old folks. But our granddaughter, Kimberlee, will be here. She is a joy."

"She'll come without her mother?" Karen asked.

Claudia chuckled, "You must think I'm younger than I look. Kimberlee is thirty and has been driving for years."

Karen looked surprised but didn't say anything, except, "What time on Thursday, if we can come?"

"Let's say three o'clock," Claudia replied.

"Wednesday night would be too late to get back to you. I'll talk to Mike and call you tomorrow."

"Perfect."

Karen didn't get up. "Claudia, before I go, can I ask one more question?"

"What is it, dear?"

"You said Kings are 'baked' and can't be changed. Does that mean they can't be changed at all?"

Claudia could see why she would ask this—Karen's husband was about to come out of the oven.

"Men continue to grow and evolve after they become Kings. But that is something they do to themselves. Kings will react poorly to being treated like a project that a woman wants to rehabilitate. In other words, don't try to change who he is. But that is different than behavior. There are many behaviors that can be changed. It is tricky and involves things you don't know, but it's possible."

"Jeez, Claudia. The more I learn from you the more there is to learn!"

Claudia nodded her head. "That is my dilemma, my dear. Before I started talking about it, I had forgotten how one idea would lead to another."

"But we're not done with the stages, are we?" Karen asked hesitantly.

Claudia shook her head. "Not quite. But it has gone a bit faster than I originally thought. I think we'll be finished in two or three more sessions."

Karen gasped, "That soon?"

Claudia nodded. Karen exclaimed, "But...but...I don't think I'm ready to do this without you!"

Claudia patted her hand again. "If you have to, you'll do just fine, honey. You'll do just fine."

Color in a Black and White World

"Hi Burt, it's Karen, is Claudia there?"

"Sure, Karen," he said warmly. In a moment she heard Claudia's voice. She hadn't noticed before how young she sounded.

"Hi Karen, how are you?" Claudia asked.

"Pretty good, actually. I wanted to get back to you about Thanksgiving. Good news; we can come."

"Oh, wonderful. I'm so glad."

"Is three o'clock still good? Can we bring anything?" Karen asked.

"Three is fine, dear. Do you bake?"

"A little, what did you have in mind? Pies?" Karen asked. She hoped not. She had never mastered pies.

"Actually, I'm already making a pecan pie, Burt's favorite. Other than that, we prefer chocolate. Can you bring brownies?" Karen laughed. Claudia had surprised her again—no stuffy traditional dinner for her.

"We love brownies. That's perfect. Anything else?"

"Actually, yes. But not about Thanksgiving," Claudia said.

"What is it?"

"Remember yesterday we were talking about receiving?"

Karen chuckled. "How could I forget? I keep noticing how terrible I am at it."

Now Claudia chuckled. "That is as good a place to start as any, Karen. Actually, I have a recommendation for you. A movie to watch."

"Really? What movie?"

"*Pretty Woman* with Julia Roberts and Richard Gere," she replied.

Karen snorted involuntarily. "Do I have to?"

She heard Claudia's serious reply. "You don't have to, obviously, but the Julia Roberts character is masterful at receiving. Watch her let his gifts inside her. See the way her body absorbs them. And you can see how a King, who is used to be taken from, responds to being received from."

"Okay, Claudia, I'll rent it and watch it before Wednesday."

"Now there's a good student," Claudia teased. "See you at yoga."

"Goodbye."

Claudia enjoyed the yoga class even more than usual. Since she had gradually become able to perform the moves and positions along with the instructor, following along required less concentration on her body. She was using the time like a meditation to mentally prepare herself for the conversation she had planned with Karen afterwards. As she moved and breathed consciously, she felt herself grow calm and centered.

As she and Karen settled in the corner of the coffee house, she noticed that Karen seemed less than enthusiastic. "Karen, are you feeling well? You don't seem quite yourself tonight."

Karen nodded and looked at Claudia with her big, golden brown eyes. Claudia doubted if Karen knew how much her eyes revealed.

"I'm feeling fine physically. I mean, I'm not sick or anything. I'm just worried about this receiving business. I watched *Pretty Woman* last night and I can't imagine myself being that open and that vulnerable."

Claudia understood completely, and she was impressed. What a perfect way to start the conversation, she thought.

"I'm glad you watched that movie. And you saw one of the most important aspects of receiving. Most people don't perceive how vulnerable that character is. But that is the essence of receiving. To fully receive the gifts life and men and other people offer us, we have to open ourselves. We have to open our hearts and let the gifts and the spirit of the giver enter. This is why the ability to receive, paradoxically, is a gift to those trying to give to us. Giving cannot occur without a receiver to allow it."

Claudia waited and watched Karen digest this. "And receiving is one the most important aspects of femininity that a woman must develop to get along with a King."

Karen seemed surprised. "Receiving is an aspect of femininity? How so?"

Claudia smiled. "That is exactly the topic I have planned for tonight. I want to talk to you about femininity. Understanding and developing and consciously expressing your femininity are one of the keys to the kingdom. And since your King is about to inhabit the kingdom, there is no time to waste!"

Karen responded to Claudia's enthusiasm. She pulled out her note pad and pen and wrote down what Claudia had just said.

"Before I start," Claudia said, "did you talk to Mike about Kings?"

Karen shook her head. "He asked me about our session on Saturday; he's always interested in what we talk about. But telling him about Kings didn't seem like the right thing to do. It could interfere with his weekend. I wanted him to have that experience without thinking about a certain place he should get to."

Claudia was surprised and pleased. "That was wise of you. And generous."

"Generous?"

"Yes, generous. The tendency is to want to control another person's experience of something. Then you can make sure it turns out the way you want. It is generous of you to allow him his own process and not try to shape it to your ends. I predict you will be rewarded for that."

Karen smiled wistfully. "I think one of the things I have learned from you is to trust Mike more. To trust his love and his intentions. By doing that I don't have to control every move anymore."

She continued, "So I didn't tell Mike about Kings, per se. I did tell him about needing to learn how to receive better. He sure got a chuckle out of that. He said I've taken self-sufficiency to a new high in the last ten years."

"What did he mean by that?" Claudia asked.

"He said that there is very little I will let him do for me. He also said I probably think I don't deserve it."

Claudia nodded knowingly. "Ah, yes. Those are two ideas that get in the way of receiving. On the one hand, women are often proving they can do everything themselves, and they won't allow anyone else to take care of them. And on the other hand, they worry about deserving what people offer, so, again, they can't accept it. Because they think they don't deserve it, accepting the gift would create an obligation they don't want. Of course, if they knew that deserving and receiving have no business with each other, they would be better off."

Karen looked puzzled. "What do you mean, 'deserving and receiving have no business with each other'?"

Claudia sipped her tea and thought about how to explain this. "What I mean is that they are two completely different things and shouldn't get mixed up together. When you deserve something that means you have earned it. A gift is something you haven't earned. That is what makes it a gift. If you had earned them, for example, people would give you your birthday compensations. But people give birthday gifts, to acknowledge and appreciate you. Gifts are never earned. They are not given because they are owed. Gifts are given because the giver is moved to give them. Gifts are an expression of the giver, not an expected result of some act or quality of the receiver. Therefore, to worry about deserving a gift is silly. You can't deserve them; it is impossible."

Karen didn't look happy about this news. "So all those times that I said, 'I can't accept that. I don't deserve it.' I was being silly?"

"Yep, a real Silly Billy," Claudia teased.

"What should I have done?" Karen asked.

Claudia responded, "Take the other point of view, and you will see. Have you ever tried to give someone something and been turned down with those same words, 'I don't deserve it'?"

Karen nodded. "Sure, plenty of times."

"Well, how did that feel to you? What do you wish the person had done instead?"

Claudia waited while Karen thought about her question. This wasn't exactly a linear way to talk about femininity, but then, she thought, femininity itself isn't linear.

Karen said, "I'm thinking of a time I found the perfect present for my mother. There was no occasion, I just saw this beautiful, tiny porcelain vase and I knew she would love it. When I gave it to her, she pushed it back towards me and said, 'No, honey, you keep it. I don't deserve that.' I felt disappointed, and a little angry. I wanted her to have it and I felt…rejected."

"And what do wish your mother had done?"

"I wish she had taken it from me and marveled at it. And asked me where I found it and what made me think of her. I wish she had noticed it, and noticed me giving it to her."

Claudia grinned.

"What?" Karen asked.

Claudia smiled at her student. "I appreciate the way that you think about things and can describe your thoughts and feelings."

"Well, thank you, but is that why you were grinning?" Karen asked.

"Actually, I was grinning because in one sentence you captured the nature of receiving. First, that you wanted your mother to 'notice' the gift and the giver. Remember, Saturday we talked about noticing being the heart of receiving?"

Karen nodded.

Claudia continued, "Second, that when we refuse to receive, under the guise of 'I don't deserve it,' our concern is all about ourselves. We're paying attention to our own embarrassment or discomfort or fear of creating an obligation, when we could be paying attention to the generosity and the communication of the giver and the gift."

"So, you're telling me that *not* receiving is *selfish* and *receiving* is *generous*?" Karen asked.

Claudia smiled again and she could feel her eyes tearing up. In that moment, the regard and compassion she felt for her student turned to love. She took a sip of tea and a deep, satisfied breath.

"Yes, Karen, that is exactly it. And brilliantly deduced, I might add. That is the paradox of receiving. Yet another thing in life that is not what it seems."

Claudia waited while Karen made some notes. The notes reminded her again of Karen's desire to teach other women, and she let herself consider it for a moment. Immediately, she thought of Kimberlee and her heart ached. But what if there is a way? she wondered for the first time. With that, a tiny bud of hope lodged itself in her mind.

Karen finished writing and looked up. "I love all this information about receiving. But what does it have to do with femininity?"

"Receiving is one of the most important capacities of the Queen," Claudia replied matter-of-factly.

"The Queen? You mean Mike is becoming a King and I have to become a Queen?" Karen asked. Her eyes opened wide and she appeared horrified. "How will I *do* that?"

Claudia patted her shoulder. "Not to worry, dear. It is more a matter of *expressing* the Queen than *becoming* the Queen. The Queen is an aspect of femininity inherent in all women. But few express her. This is why I think Mike's weekend away is good for you too. It will give you the time and room to begin working on the Queen that you are."

"But how do I do that?" Karen inquired again, still sounding distressed.

"Let's start at the beginning—this is going to take awhile, though. Would you like a refill on your coffee? Would you mind getting me some more tea?"

While Karen refilled their beverages, Claudia thought about how to explain femininity to Karen. Funny, she thought, I never have to explain femininity to men. They know more about femininity than women do.

Karen returned and settled in again. "You usually don't stay this late after yoga. Are you sure this is okay? Tomorrow is going to be a big day."

Claudia nodded at Karen's reference to Thanksgiving. "Yes, I'm excited about having you and Mike over. I'll get to meet Mike and you'll get to meet my granddaughter, Kimberlee."

"But it's a lot of work for you, isn't it?"

Claudia smiled. "I have been preparing Thanksgiving dinner for fifty-five years; I have it down to a science. It will be practically effortless."

Karen looked skeptical. "Fifty-five years? Did you start as a child?"

Claudia smiled again. "Well, of course, I helped my mother and grandmother as a child. But I am referring to my life since I got married."

Now Karen looked shocked. "You've been married for *fifty-five years*? Were you *ten*?"

Claudia chuckled. "How old do you think I am, dear?"

Karen hesitated. "I figured you were about sixty-five."

"And what made you think that?" Claudia asked.

Karen hesitated again. "Well…because you're playful, I guess."

This made Claudia grin; it was as if Karen was reading a script that provided opening lines for Claudia to teach her. "Well, I appreciate that, dear. It is good to know one is aging well. The quality you are talking about—playfulness—is a quality of femininity. It is important for women to not lose their playfulness, no matter how old they get."

Karen asked tentatively, "So, are you going to tell me? How old *are* you?"

"I turned seventy-seven at the end of September."

Karen's face clearly showed her surprise. Claudia was delighted.

"Can we move on now?" she asked, teasingly.

Karen nodded, speechless.

"Femininity could be described as certain special qualities inherent in women. Obviously, they can also be found in men, just as masculine qualities can be found in women. But we're not working on that right now. For now, understand that there are particular qualities of femininity that exist inside every woman as a *potential*. Whether or not she expresses these qualities is ultimately up to her. No matter how she was raised, as an adult she can choose what to nurture, develop and express. She just needs to understand what the qualities are and how to nurture them."

Karen was furiously taking notes. She asked, "What qualities are you referring to?"

Claudia answered, "I have already mentioned playfulness and receptivity, or the ability to receive. But there are many others—too many to mention, in fact."

"Can you just give me a few? To get me started?"

Claudia nodded. "Sure. But let's take them in groups."

Karen interjected, "In groups? What do you mean?"

Claudia explained, "Men respond to feminine qualities in particular, predictable ways. It is helpful to group the qualities together by the way that men respond to them. For example, the qualities of playfulness and sexuality and sensuality. Men respond to these with participation—they inspire a man to participate with a woman. They affect men of all ages the same. Like your student, Casey. Have you noticed that the more playful you are with him, the more he wants to participate with you?"

Karen sipped her coffee and Claudia waited patiently. "I think you're right. When I kid around with him—in a nice way, not a mean way—he seems to like it. He blushes but he moves towards me, not away from me."

Claudia was pleased again. "Very good. The point you made about 'in a nice way' is important. Men tease each other in a sort of brutal, sometimes truthful, sometimes exaggerating way. And it makes women think they can do the same—but they can't. From a woman, it is cutting. This is why it is important to be playful and teasing with kindness and affection."

She continued, "The other thing I like about what you said is how you noticed he moves toward you instead of away. You can tell a lot from a man's body. You have to know what to watch for but when you do, their feelings are often obvious."

Karen perked up. "Can you tell me more about that?"

Claudia smiled; Karen was always hungry for her information. After Myra's rebellious disinterest, Claudia needed that.

"I bet you have seen a lot of it with Casey, already. And maybe with Mike. Have you noticed either one of them seeming to grow larger before your very eyes?"

Karen nodded enthusiastically. "Oh yes! I see that with Casey when I'm impressed by him. He kind of puffs his chest out."

Claudia nodded and smiled. "Yes, exactly. We have always called that 'puffing up' because that is what it looks like. Their chests swell and their shoulders go up and back and they look bigger."

"But what is it that they are feeling when that happens?" Karen asked.

"Happiness and power."

"Happiness and power?" Karen repeated.

Claudia nodded. "Yes. Absolutely. That is what they look like when they are happy and feel powerful. The two qualities go together; men derive power from happiness. On the other hand, when they have been diminished in some way, they also show it physically—they slump or shrink. That is what they look like when they have been disempowered."

Karen wrote quickly. "Can you tell me anything else?"

Claudia thought about it. "Well, just one more, because we have a lot more femininity to cover. Have you ever noticed that when you appreciate a man for something, he doesn't say much? He doesn't gush about it or go on the way a woman would?"

Karen smiled sadly, "Well, until recently, I haven't had much experience appreciating men. But I did notice that when I thanked Mike for how hard he has worked for us, I didn't get much of a reaction."

Claudia nodded. "Watch me closely. Was it something like this?" In the smallest movement, she raised her shoulders and moved them backwards a fraction, slightly stiffening her neck at the same time.

"What did you do? I didn't see anything."

"Watch again, carefully," Claudia said and repeated the movement.

"I saw it!" Karen exclaimed. "But what was that?"

"That is how a man looks when he is deeply affected by an acknowledgment. It means that it mattered to him to be thanked for that. It is a sign of feeling recognized."

Karen was shaking her head. "Wow. I never would have thought. That is exactly what Mike did."

"Well, that tells you that what you thanked him for was important to him."

Karen was still shaking her head. Her next comment took Claudia by surprise. "You probably don't even know how much you know about men."

Claudia smiled. "You ask the questions, I reach for the answers. And they are just there. I've been feeling a little like an encyclopedia."

"Well, thank goodness for that. When I think about how it was with Mike and me a few weeks ago, and how it is now...You've got a million dollar encyclopedia in there." Karen smiled at her and Claudia could feel her appreciation. She reminded herself to breathe and receive.

"It is my pleasure. You're most welcome," she said graciously.

Karen exclaimed, "That's it! Right there! That was the Queen, wasn't it?"

Claudia smiled and chuckled, "You are a sharp one, that's for sure." She watched as Karen first began to object, caught herself, took a breath and said, "Thank you."

"Good. See, it's not so bad, is it?"

Karen nodded. "It's a little uncomfortable but I lived through it."

Claudia smiled. "And since we are in yoga class together, we can talk about energy. Did you notice that with me receiving the gift you offered and you receiving the gift I offered, that the energy kept flowing?"

Karen looked thoughtful. She said, "Now that you mention it, yes. It flowed and it grew. Does the opposite happen when people won't receive?"

"Yessiree, Bob," Claudia stated matter-of-factly.

Karen laughed. "'Silly Billy' and 'Yessiree, Bob'—Did you grow up in the South? You don't have much of an accent, if you did, but you sure have some interesting expressions."

Claudia felt warmed by Karen's remark. No matter how old we get, she thought, we still want to be special and we still want to be noticed.

"Actually, I was born and raised in California. But my mother's family had lived in the South since before the Civil War."

Karen suddenly exclaimed, "Oh, I just remembered! Can I tell you about something?"

"Certainly, dear. What is it?"

"Since today was the last day before the holiday weekend, you can probably imagine how the kids were. Finding a teachable millisecond was difficult, let alone a string of teachable moments."

Claudia nodded her understanding.

"So I gave up and put in a video for the kids to watch. I was doing paperwork when all of sudden I heard the little lion, Simba, singing about being a king. Do you know the movie I'm talking about? *The Lion King*?"

Claudia nodded enthusiastically. She guessed what Karen was going to say next.

"That movie is about the Stages of Development, isn't it?" Karen said excitedly.

Claudia shook her head. "We have no way of knowing if the writers intended it to be that way, but you certainly can see all of the stages, can't you? I love that movie; I should have thought to tell you to see it."

"Well, after that, I watched the whole thing with the kids. It was fascinating. I think it even had a version of the Tunnel in it. But what stage was the baboon? What's his name? I couldn't figure that one out."

"His name is Rafiki. You couldn't figure it out because we haven't talked about it. Rafiki is an Elder."

"An Elder?" Karen asked.

"An Elder. It is not actually a stage. It is a state that some Kings enter. It is more like a completely different kind of person. They are not compelled by the same things that compel other men. The easiest way to think of them is as the wise men in the community. They are insightful and humble and serve humanity in their own ways."

"Is Burt an Elder?" Karen asked.

Claudia smiled and nodded, glad Karen had noticed. "Yes, he is. And if you remind me tomorrow, I'll give you something that an Elder once wrote about being an Elder. It is quite profound."

"Did Burt write it?"

"No," she said. "A dear, special friend wrote it. His gift is with words; Burt's gift is with wood. Let's get back to femininity, shall we?"

Karen looked reluctant but took up her pen again. "Yep, what other qualities are hidden inside me? Do I have ESP?"

Claudia chuckled. "No, but something close to it. It's called 'compassion.' It is the ability to enter into another person's world—whether it is their emotions or mental state or even physical experience—and see what it is like to be them. It can feel like ESP. For a moment you feel like you *are* them. Do you know what I mean?"

Karen looked thoughtful, then nodded. "Yes, I do, it's happened from time to time. It's kind of freaky. I remember watching a man cross the street and all of a sudden, for a moment, I felt his coat as if it was on my shoulders."

Claudia leaned forward. "It is only 'freaky' if you don't understand it. It's one of the completely normal and magical things women can do."

"You said 'normal' and 'magical' in the same sentence!" Karen exclaimed. "How can you do that with a straight face?"

Claudia laughed. "Because I understand femininity, that's how."

Karen was shaking her head as she wrote. She looked up, "Okay, say more. Lay it on me."

Claudia laughed again; this was turning out to be much more fun than she had anticipated. "Compassion is integral to femininity. All expressions of femininity need compassion to inform them."

"Inform them?"

"It's like this. The nurturing aspect of femininity—you could call it 'Mother' as an archetype—needs compassion to see what the person before her needs. Without compassion, she may assume she knows what that person needs and be far off the mark. Then she is pushy and bossy and meddling instead of nurturing and effective."

Karen was nodding and writing. "I can see what you mean. I have mothers who think they know their children well; they are sure they know what the child needs. But I spend more time with their children than they do. And I see things that make a difference with them. And then their mom will come in and do the exact opposite of what supports that child."

"That is what happens when we don't practice compassion. It is easier to raise our children like we were raised, or to raise each child the same, or to follow a book. But if a mother looks at her children with compassion, she will see what they need. Often, if a mother has three children, she will need to be three different kinds of mother. With compassion she'll be able to see the kind of nurturing each child needs."

Claudia brought herself up short. She knew she could get caught up in this subject. Then she thought of Myra. And with all the compassion a woman can muster, sometimes her children will still throw her for a loop, she thought. She remembered the circumstances that led up to Myra's near total rejection of men, and wondered for the thousandth time how she could have intervened. Even a mother's compassion couldn't help her counteract the combined influence of the 60s, free love, feminism, an unexpected pregnancy, and finally, abandonment by Kimberlee's father. With a sad sigh, Claudia forced herself back to the present.

"Let's look at compassion itself some more. If a woman is expressing the playful or sensual part of her nature, compassion will give her a delightful sensitivity to her playmate. And if a woman is being the Queen, compassion will provide the understanding she needs to influence and empower the people in her realm."

"Her 'realm'?" Karen repeated.

"Yes, her realm. A Queen's realm consists of the people to whom she is dedicated. I believe it is important to reserve our best selves, our greatest qualities, for our realm."

"Wow. I've never heard of such a thing," Karen said. "Aren't we supposed to be wonderful with everyone?"

"I know people think that. And I believe in being courteous and kind to other people. But femininity requires energy, and lots of it. If you give your nurturing and playfulness and graciousness to everyone, when you get home to the people who depend upon you, you might not have the energy to provide those qualities for them."

Claudia watched while Karen absorbed this. She could see the play of emotions across her face and knew she had struck home. Karen's eyes began to tear.

"I think Mike was trying to tell me something about this. That with all my committees and commitments I had very little left to give him. At the time I just thought he was being selfish. When we talked about him being a Prince, he mentioned something about having to wait in line."

Claudia smiled to herself. Karen continued to provide the opportunities she needed. "Men *need* femininity. They call it 'color in a black and white world.' It heals their wounds, soothes their spirits and recharges their batteries. It is one of the things men look for in their wives: someone who makes them more powerful by feeding them with their femininity. If a woman has other priorities, especially ones that tire her out, then her feminine power isn't available to her husband. He suffers for it and will resent the things that she puts before him. And it's easy to tell what he thinks comes before him, because he will attack them verbally."

Karen was shaking her head and held up her hand. "Wait a second, please. There are two things you just said that really bother me. Can we talk about them?"

Claudia nodded.

"First, you emphasized 'especially ones that tire her out.' What did you mean by that?"

Claudia answered in a level voice, "Like I said a moment ago, femininity requires energy. Without energy, we can't be feminine. We can't bring all those priceless qualities to the people we love. When we do too much and don't take care of ourselves, we have no energy to be what women can be."

Karen held her gaze as she digested this. Claudia could see the recognition in her eyes. Claudia nodded as if Karen had verbalized her understanding.

Karen's eyes narrowed. "Okay, I see that. The other thing you said was that when a wife isn't available for her husband, he suffers and resents the other things she is doing. But I thought you said women should have passions of their own. I don't get it. Am I supposed to make Mike my priority?"

Claudia tilted her head to the side. "Well, that would depend upon what you wanted."

"What do you mean?" Karen asked suspiciously.

"Of course you should have passions of your own, to not lose your sense of self. But if you want your husband to be powerful and you want your marriage to be strong, you will make him and your marriage your first priority."

"Ugh!" Karen exclaimed.

Claudia chuckled. "I know this sounds like counter-feminism, but if you listen closely, I think you'll see it's something altogether different. I am advocating you being powerful and expressed in your own right. I want you to fully understand your unique and priceless contribution. *And*, if you choose to make your partnership with your husband your first priority, you will both have access to something extraordinary and wonderful."

Karen kept shaking her head. Claudia thought this was a good time to introduce her main point.

"To further confuse you, Karen. I want you to do something this weekend in preparation for your King, perhaps out of making your partnership your first priority."

"What is it? What do you want me to do?"

"I want you to take care of yourself."

"What?" Karen said. "I thought you wanted me to do something for him."

"Yes. Exactly."

"Huh???"

Claudia smiled. "This is another one of those paradoxes. Remember how you saw that not receiving is selfish and receiving is generous?"

Karen nodded.

"Well. One of the most generous things you can do for another person is to take care of yourself."

Karen shook her head. "You've lost me."

"It's okay," Claudia replied. "If you are willing to do what I ask, then by Monday you will know exactly what I am talking about."

"What are you asking?"

"Well, let's see. Tell me some of the things that make you feel serene."

Karen frowned, then replied, "Walks on the beach, bubble baths, time alone in nature."

"Great. And what are some of the things that make you feel strong?"

Karen frowned again as she thought. "Exercise. Time outdoors. Talking to my dad. Drinking lots of water."

"Okay. And what makes you feel connected to God or Spirit?"

That question clearly surprised Karen. Claudia didn't change her demeanor.

"Time in nature, in the mountains or at the beach. Watching babies and small children. Puppies. Listening to certain music."

"Terrific. Perfect. There you are. That's what I want you to do while Mike is gone this weekend."

"All of those things?"

Claudia laughed. "If you listened to yourself, you'd see it's not all that much. The activity you get the most out of is time outdoors at the beach. You get serenity, strength and connectedness. I would recommend doing that every day this weekend. And watch the little ones play in the sand. If you did that and talked to your dad on Friday or Saturday, had a bubble bath on Sunday not too long before Mike got home, and threw in some music along the way, you'd be set."

"Set for what?" Karen asked.

"Set for being the Queen when the King returns," Claudia said simply.

Karen looked incredulous. "It's that simple?"

Claudia shook her head. "Well, not really. On an ongoing basis there are other things to consider. For example, the Queen is visionary and passionate. At some point you should think about that. And there is knowing how to take care of yourself over the long run and in times of stress. Understanding where to spend your time and energy to get the best return. But what we've talked about is a good start. It will have you ready for Mike."

Claudia looked expectantly at Karen. "So, will you do it?"

Karen didn't answer right away. Claudia appreciated that when Karen committed, one could count on it. She waited.

"I can't promise to talk to my dad, because they usually go out of town for Thanksgiving."

"Could you substitute drinking lots of water?"

Karen laughed. "That sounds funny—talk to my dad or drink lots of water. But it's true, they both make me feel strong."

She paused, then whispered, "Okay, I'll do it."

"Wonderful. I can't wait to hear what it provides for you."

Claudia gathered her purse. Karen stood up and impulsively hugged her, and Claudia responded warmly.

Karen said, "So, we'll see you tomorrow at three, right?"

Claudia smiled. "Yes! It's going to be wonderful."

Then Claudia remembered something, and grew serious. "Karen, there is something important I must ask of you."

"What is it?"

"My granddaughter has no knowledge of my ancestry, this body of knowledge, or my research. And I need it to stay that way." As she saw Karen start to interrupt, she said, "Please don't ask me to explain."

"Okay…what do you want from me?"

"I need you and Mike to not mention our work together. We need a day off from our lessons anyhow, yes? If she asks, just tell Kimberlee that we met at yoga and became friends. Would you do that for me, please? It is important to me."

Karen nodded. "Sure, Claudia, whatever you want." She joked, "I'll probably bite my tongue a thousand times and not be able to eat the turkey, though!"

Claudia appreciated Karen's attempt at humor, but couldn't bring herself to laugh. She was worried about their Thanksgiving together. While she wanted Kimberlee to meet Karen, and felt it was important to her budding plan, she didn't want anything revealed too soon.

"Thank you, Karen. I'll see you tomorrow."

As Karen entered the house, she saw that Mike was still up, TV remote in hand. She put her things down and snuggled in beside him on the couch.

"Watcha watchin'?" she asked, although it was fair to assume it would be a car-related show.

"Oh, nothing. They're all reruns tonight." He clicked off the TV and turned to her. "I'd rather talk to you. You're out late. Did you meet with Claudia tonight?"

"Yep. She wanted to get me ready for your return on Sunday. She has a funny idea that me taking care of myself is something I can do for *you*."

To her surprise, Mike immediately nodded. "Yep, that's true."

"What? You agree with her? How does my taking care of myself benefit *you*?"

His arm tightened around her. "It's simple, actually. When you're happy, I'm happy."

"Really?" Karen couldn't believe it was that straightforward.

"Pretty much. If I've had a great day and I come home and you're unhappy, I lose all my steam. On the other hand, if I've had a crappy day, and I come home and you're happy, my day fades away. After a little while of being around you, I get happy."

Karen was shaking her head. "I just can't believe I have that much of an effect on you."

Mike shook his head; it was clearly obvious to him. "You're silly, honey."

"That is the second time tonight I've been called silly!"

"Really?" Mike asked, "Who else called you silly?"

"Claudia called me a 'Silly Billy.'"

Mike laughed and shook his head. "Claudia sure sounds like a character. I was looking forward to meeting her tomorrow…but now that it's here, I must admit I'm kind of nervous."

"Nervous?" Karen asked. Why would Mike be nervous? Claudia was one of the kindest people she had ever known.

"Well, am I going to feel like a bug? Is she *always* studying men?"

Karen laughed. "I don't know. She doesn't have a scientific air about her, if that's what you mean. She's not rude or out of place. She just seems wise and compassionate. I get the impression she gathers information as she lives her life and observes people."

The concern left Mike's face. "Cool," he said.

"There *is* something about tomorrow that I need to tell you," Karen said seriously.

"What's that? You found out she's a horrible cook and we should eat before we go?" Mike joked. Karen knew he was only half-joking, though; good food was important to him.

"No, that's not it. I think dinner will be great. Maybe a little eclectic; we're bringing brownies. I've never had brownies after Thanksgiving dinner."

Karen adjusted herself to look directly at Mike. "Claudia asked that we not mention any of the work she and I have done together. She wants us to say that we met at yoga and became friends."

Mike frowned. "That sounds strange. From what you've told me about her, she sounds like a straight shooter. Why would she have you conceal something like that?"

Karen shook her head. "I don't know. She wouldn't explain except to say that Kimberlee—that's her granddaughter—doesn't know anything about her gender research. She always looks pained whenever her daughter or granddaughter come up. I try not to push."

"Interesting. Bet there's a good story in there," Mike commented. "So, are you going to tell me about Kings yet?"

His question caught her off guard. She decided to go with the truth, and suddenly remembered making that promise to herself after her first session with Claudia. Was that only four weeks ago? She noticed how comfortably she and Mike were sitting together and talking. The tension was gone, replaced by easy companionship and a sense of sharing. Impulsively, she kissed him warmly on the cheek and sat back and looked at him.

"I haven't been telling you about Kings because I want you to feel free to experience your weekend. I don't want you to feel like something has to happen down in San Diego. Like you have to come home a King."

Mike smiled a little. "Thanks. I appreciate that. I have no idea what is going to happen."

Unexpectedly, Mike leaned forward and nuzzled her ear. He spoke to her neck, his voice sounding husky, "Remember when we watched *American Beauty*?"

She nodded slightly, not wanting him to move away. "Uh huh…"

"You know the scene where Annette Bening cries out, 'You are the King!'"

Karen could feel herself blushing and warming as she remembered. "Yeah…"

He tickled her neck with his nose. "Do I have to be a King first for you to do that?" he asked, now kissing her neck.

A moan escaped her lips. What a great way to start a holiday weekend, she thought.

Much to Be Thankful For

As they neared Claudia's house, Mike admired the neighborhood of old bungalow-style homes. The trees on Claudia's street were large and mature, adding to the feeling of history and security. Claudia's house was a medium blue-gray with cheerful white trim. As they stood at the front door, he checked out the underside of the porch roof. The eaves were finished and painted white too. Baskets full of flowers and miniature trailing ivy hung from the eaves, subtly boasting about the sunny southern California weather. He had always loved the wide front porches of these houses. He admired the comfortable white wicker chairs and small table facing the street. This porch looked cheerful, comfortable and lived-in.

When Claudia answered the door, Mike was immediately impressed by her vitality. Karen had told him her age but he found it hard to believe. Claudia's bright blue eyes welcomed him with a twinkle and he liked her instantly, which was fortunate since he already felt deeply indebted to her. He handed her the bouquet of flowers they had brought and was thanked with a squeeze on the arm.

As they entered the living room, he noticed a young woman seated on the couch and knew she must be Claudia's granddaughter. Even from a distance, he could see that her eyes were the same distinctive blue and saw the resemblance in the shape of their faces. Both had high cheekbones, wide smiles and deep dimples. As he shook Kimberlee's hand, he realized that the biggest difference between grandmother and granddaughter wasn't age or wrinkles. Where Claudia's face was soft and welcoming, Kimberlee's was sharp and edgy. The hard line of her jaw was further accentuated by her short dark hair. Although attractive in form, she seemed tough and masculine, like many of the women he knew.

He looked over at Karen and noted a softness in her face that was new. She used to look more like Kimberlee, he thought. How interesting. Now she looks more open, more inviting, and more approachable. He smiled to himself remembering how, lately, he couldn't prevent himself from approaching.

As he stepped through the French doors in search of Burt, he surveyed the backyard. So this is the garden where it all happens, he thought. To the left he saw the famous table and chairs on a foundation of old brick. They were placed on a narrow strip of grass raised about two feet higher than the rest of the yard. It must be a lovely view, he thought.

To the right, and perpendicular to the house, was a separate building that he assumed was Burt's woodshop. He hoped he'd get to see inside. He was curious about Burt's work and had always wanted his own workshop.

Before him lay a kidney-shaped stretch of lawn surrounded by beds full of abundant leafy green perennials and a few flowers still in bloom. Not a bare spot to be seen. He assumed these beds would blossom profusely in the spring. The large yard was surrounded by tall, vine-covered fences, with a grand old oak providing shade from the south.

Mike was pleased. The entire space looked loved and lived-in. The only thing he would change, he thought, would be to put a bench tucked in the right curve of the lawn, looking back at the house and seating area. That's where he would be found, with the sun at his back on a lazy day.

Burt came out of his shop just then, wiping his hands on the front of his coveralls. In contrast to Claudia's petite size, Burt was tall and thickly built. He reminded Mike of a grizzled old bear. Burt crossed the distance on the brick path and shook Mike's hand. The carpenter's hand felt rough and strong and had the residue of something like sawdust.

Apparently noticing it himself, Burt wiped his hand on his thigh and apologized. "Sorry, Mike. I should be all washed up and spiffy by now.

But my project is so close to being finished, I can't help but sneak out here and work on it." Burt smiled mischievously and winked at Mike.

Mike smiled back and felt right at home. Burt was what they called a "man's man." Knowing Claudia was seventy-seven, he guessed Burt must be pushing eighty. But he didn't seem twice Mike's age. He wasn't patronizing or standoffish, or remote the way some older people are; he seemed like a regular guy. Mike relaxed some more and began to look forward to spending the holiday here.

"Do you mind if I leave you here and make myself presentable?" Burt asked. "Lucky for me Claudia never nags, or I'd be in trouble for being late to the party."

Mike chuckled. Within moments of meeting him, Burt had already given Mike a view of his life. "Sure. This is beautiful. Mind if I walk around?"

"Nothing would make Claudia happier. But don't ask her for a tour or we'll never have dinner!" the older man bellowed.

Burt turned towards the house. He must have noticed Mike looking longingly at his shop, because he turned back and said, "I'll show you the shop later, while the ladies are busy talking. I can't let *them* see what I'm doing yet." He winked again and walked away whistling. Mike thought it sounded like the theme from *Popeye the Sailor Man.*

Mike headed for the southwest end of the garden to see if the view from his imaginary bench was as nice as he thought it would be. After that, he planned on visiting the table and chairs. Karen must have told him twenty times that he *had* to see them.

As Burt entered the house, Kimberlee caught his attention.

"Hi, Sweetheart," he exclaimed. "My, aren't you just a vision. Can I have a squeeze?"

He met Kimberlee halfway and gave her a warm embrace. He noticed her face soften a little, and thought, this girl is not being hugged enough.

Immediately, he saw her flicking tiny wood chips off her pretty blue sweater. "Oh, I'm sorry. I should have changed my clothes first. I'll be out in a jiffy. Lovely to see you, honey."

As Burt crossed the living room, he didn't notice the look of wonder on Kimberlee's face.

Claudia was busy in the kitchen. No matter how much one did in advance, there was no avoiding that last hour of activity after the turkey came out of the oven to rest, and the gravy and mashed potatoes had to be made. She was glad Karen was helpful, and put her in charge of the potatoes. She saw Kimberlee looking a little uncomfortable and asked her to arrange the flowers from Karen and Mike for the table. She handed her a large crystal vase and a pair of scissors.

"Where is Mike?" Claudia asked.

Karen looked out the window behind the breakfast booth, towards the yard. "He seems to be surveying your backyard."

"Does your husband enjoy gardening?" Kimberlee asked. Claudia was glad she had included herself.

"Actually Mike is fascinated by the use of space. He may be planning a remodel for you, Claudia," Karen joked.

"He's in construction?" Kimberlee inquired.

Karen's response was warm and friendly toward Kimberlee, and Claudia started to relax. "He has his own construction company. He specializes in large custom homes." She paused. "Or, at least, he has. The way he's been talking recently, it seems like a change is in the works."

"What do you mean?" Kimberlee asked as she cut the ends off the flowers.

Claudia paused in mid-stir, then continued, hoping no one noticed. She need not have worried, she realized, as Karen answered.

"He's been doing a lot of thinking lately and he keeps complaining that the houses he builds are," Karen lowered her voice in an imitation of Mike, "'a waste of space and natural resources.'" Then she added in her normal voice, "I'm not sure what that means about the future."

Kimberlee surprised Claudia when she asked Karen, "Doesn't that worry you? Not knowing what is going to happen?"

Karen shrugged easily. "Mike and I have been through a lot in twenty years. I'm sure we can handle whatever's next."

Kimberlee seemed surprised. "You've been married for that long?" she asked.

"Why? Is that a surprise? We've been together since college," Karen replied.

Kimberlee was shaking her head. She began arranging the colorful fall flowers in the crystal vase.

"I just assumed you were newlyweds or something."

"What made you think that?" Karen asked gently.

Claudia appreciated how Karen was interacting with Kimberlee. She was used to her granddaughter's direct, somewhat interrogative way of speaking. It was masculine and she knew where the career woman had acquired it. She was relieved that Karen responded with softness.

She noticed Kimberlee shift nervously from one foot to the other. She kept arranging the flowers and didn't turn around. "Well, I noticed the way he looks at you. You don't usually see that in long-term couples." She added, jokingly, "Except my grandparents, of course, but they're weird."

"What way is that, Kimberlee?" Karen asked, even more gently.

Claudia reminded herself to keep breathing.

"Like he's in love with you."

Claudia kept stirring the gravy as if nothing unusual was happening. Serenity, she thought, practice serenity. Karen couldn't have been more perfect if Claudia had included her in her developing plan.

Karen replied softly, "Well, that's a really nice thing to say."

Claudia sensed that Karen would have liked to say more. Karen glanced over at her and smoothly changed the subject. Claudia counted this as the first tongue-biting Karen would have to endure that day, and was deeply grateful.

"Kimberlee, that's wonderful what you've done with those mums. You're so creative."

"Ah, 'tweren't nothin'," Kimberlee responded in a mock hillbilly accent, expertly dodging the compliment. As she took the flowers to the dining room, Karen looked at Claudia and winked. Claudia closed her eyes and shook her head, half-smiling.

When Kimberlee returned, she looked quickly around and asked in a whisper, "Grandmother, what's up with Granddad? He seems *chipper*. Do you have him on new vitamins or something?"

Claudia smiled. "Seems like it, doesn't it? Actually, he has a new project. I've been pretending not to notice, but I think tonight would be a good time to start asking him about it."

"Do you know what it is?"

"Nope. It's some big surprise he's been planning for the last few weeks. He spends hours in his shop. At first he emerged covered in sawdust; now, it's mostly tiny wood chips. That means he must be carving something. And the most telltale sign: He keeps whistling *I'm Popeye the Sailor Man*. He hasn't done that much in the last ten years."

Burt pushed himself back from the table and sighed, "Sweetheart, you did it again. That was wonderful."

Claudia beamed back at him. "You're welcome, honey."

"Hmm. What should we do next?" he asked. "Dessert? Or maybe Mike would like to see my shop first?" He saw Mike's face brighten.

"That'd be great, Burt," Mike responded. "Is that alright with you ladies?"

During dinner, the ladies had made numerous inquiries regarding Burt's project. He loved the attention but made it clear that it was a surprise. Claudia had remarked that he hadn't spent this much time on a project since he completed the table and chairs.

"The table and chairs?" Kimberlee had asked.

"Yes, dear," Claudia had replied, "the table and chairs in the garden."

"Oh," Kimberlee had said. "Now I remember. The one with the roses around the edge."

Burt had seen Karen and Claudia exchange a look but no one contradicted her.

Back in the present, the men were negotiating their independence. Since the ladies would not be included in their excursion, Burt was glad Mike was being diplomatic, although he knew it wasn't necessary for Claudia.

Claudia winked at Burt. "Well, since we're not allowed in the woodshed..."

Suddenly Burt bellowed, "Woodshed! It's not a woodshed! That's where you keep *firewood*. Mine is a *workshop*. Where I create *works of art!*"

Claudia appeared aghast but couldn't keep it going. She giggled and grinned. "I love it when you react like that. It works even after fifty years."

"Fifty years?" Mike asked.

Burt laughed too. "Let me explain. Okay, Claudia?"

She smiled and nodded.

Warming himself to one of his favorite stories, he said, "About fifty years ago, when we bought this house, I told Claudia that what I wanted was a place to do my woodworking. I needed a private place where my materials and the sawdust and wood chips wouldn't be disturbed by the children. So, as a surprise, Claudia spoke to my boss about his company building it for me. Only, Claudia told him that what I needed was a *woodshed!* Frank could not figure out why we would need a general contractor to build a woodshed. He finally asked me about it. It spoiled Claudia's surprise, but thank goodness!" he finished, laughing.

Claudia smiled at him, mischievously. "So, Mike," she said, glancing sideways at Burt and back at Mike, "would you like to see Burt's fancy woodshed?"

"I would love to!" Mike laughed. "Can we have dessert when we get back?"

Claudia nodded.

"What's for dessert, by the way?" Mike asked.

Claudia said, teasingly, "Nope, you fellas have your surprise, and we have ours."

As he and Burt walked across the brick path to the "woodshed," the cool night air felt refreshing. Burt opened the door and welcomed him inside. Mike looked around enviously. The entire room appeared to be about 400 square feet. To the left was a wide workbench with tools hanging neatly on either side of the broad window. To the right was a collection of wood carefully stacked and organized by size and type of wood. The back wall appeared to be an insulated garage door. Knowing now how much Burt liked surprises, Mike guessed that this allowed Burt to bring his materials in covertly. The smell of wood and iron, tools and sweat combined sweetly in Mike's nostrils. He took a deep breath and relaxed the way a man can in a man's world.

Then he spotted it and his mouth fell open. After several long moments, he looked over at Burt in awe. Burt swelled up and grinned at him. In that moment, the older man looked twenty years younger.

Mike approached the bench. "Can I touch it?"

Burt nodded. "Just the parts that are stained, though."

Mike nodded, understanding perfectly. He wouldn't want to imbed the wood with the oil in his fingertips. He reached out and touched the seat of the bench, running his hand along the butter-smooth surface. He admired the grain and loved the dark brown stain; it would go perfectly with the table and chairs. The surface was expertly sealed against the elements. He noticed the seat was not flat, but curved for greater comfort.

He continued his inspection along the arms, which were also stained, sealed and butter-smooth. They also curved, this time for both comfort and beauty.

Finally, he turned his attention to the most astonishing part of all, the seat back. He inspected it the way he would one of his own construction jobs. He noticed that, while the seat back was carved, it was done in such a way that when someone leaned back, they would feel only smooth surfaces. The carving itself was recessed even at its highest points. Very clever. While he examined the bench, his praise was expressed only in "ahhhh" repeated over and over again. Out of the corner of his eye, he could see Burt smiling as he stood with his legs wide and his arms crossed over his chest victoriously.

After he had closely examined the workmanship, he stepped back to appreciate the carving itself. What a marvel. It was a mural, of sorts, which started to the left and continued to the right across the seat back. It consisted of five scenes, about one square foot each, with a sense of one flowing into the other. How do you create movement in wood? he wondered.

The first scene was of a boy standing at the side of a horse. The horse was mounted, but only the leg of the rider was shown and the top of the scene ended at the rider's waist. The boy was holding up a huge sword for the rider to accept. The boy was straining under the sword's weight but there was also pride in the profile of his face.

The second scene showed another horse and rider. This time it was obviously the boy grown into a young man. His sword was raised as he and his horse charged off into some unseen adventure. The sun glinted off the edge of the sword.

The third scene showed the back of the horse and rider at the bottom of a tall mountain. A winding trail was visible from the bottom of the mountain almost to the top. There was the distinct impression that the horse and rider were starting up the mountain and it was going to be a long haul. The sword was sheathed and there was a small crown atop the rider's head.

In the fourth scene, the boy's face was now clearly a grown man's. It was weathered and experienced and very certain. His jaw was set and his shoulders were back. He sat upon a heavy throne and wore a large crown.

In the fifth scene, the man was now elderly. He had a long beard and wizened features. He sat in a large, comfortable chair with children gathered at his feet. He looked happy and peaceful.

Mike looked at each scene in turn and then started back at the beginning.

"Wow," he finally said. "Claudia's going to flip."

He blinked the water from his eyes and said simply, "It's beautiful."

After another long pause while he gazed at the mural, he asked, "Is this for that spot to the right in the garden?"

"Yes," Burt replied.

"That will be perfect. I was wondering why you didn't have a bench there."

Burt nodded. "We used to. Something we bought decades ago. But Claudia didn't want ordinary garden furniture to share the space with her table and chairs. And I haven't had both the desire and the energy to make something like this. At least, not until recently."

"Recently?"

"When Claudia started teaching Karen, she became more alive. She has energy and purpose. It feeds me. As soon as she decided to teach Karen, I wanted to make the bench. As I've heard about the Stages of Development, I knew what I had to put on it."

Mike responded, "I recognize all but the last one. What is that?"

"It's called 'Elder.' It is when a man's life is complete. There is nothing to do but enjoy life, explore what you are curious about, appreciate your blessings, and serve humanity."

"That's you, isn't it?" Mike said in awe.

"Yes. That's me."

Mike was puzzled. Since he didn't know enough about Burt to answer it himself, he ventured a question. "Can I ask? How do you serve humanity?"

He watched as Burt considered his answer. Finally, the Elder said, "By serving Claudia."

"Claudia?" Mike was confused.

"Claudia."

After a pause, Burt elaborated. "Claudia has an important contribution to make to humanity. I serve humanity by making sure her contribution will be made."

Mike was thoughtful. "Karen told me that Claudia doesn't want to teach anyone else. And Claudia's only planning on teaching Karen a fraction of what she knows."

Burt said, "See, I have my work cut out for me, don't I?" He smiled good-naturedly.

Mike shook his head in wonder. He said, seriously, "If there's any way that I can help, you got it. Okay? I owe you."

Burt nodded and patted Mike's shoulder. "Thanks, Mike. You and Karen being here today has already helped. If Claudia can figure out a way to teach Kimberlee, that will be the real beginning."

"What has to happen for her to teach Kimberlee?"

Burt was thoughtful. "I haven't asked Claudia that specifically. But I suspect that Kimberlee has to open her heart."

From just a few short hours with Kimberlee, Mike knew exactly what Burt was talking about. He thought about Karen a few weeks ago. Though upset and hurt and lost, her heart was still open. Claudia must have recognized that.

"How has our being here helped?" Mike asked.

"From what Claudia whispered to me about the conversation in the kitchen, I think you have helped by showing her that it is possible."

"That what is possible?"

"Well, Kimberlee noticed a long time ago that Claudia and I are in love. But she discounted us—like we're an interesting exception to the rule. Today, she saw that two people closer to her own age have that too."

Mike was stunned. *In love?* Shaking his head in recognition, he laughed.

"Yes?" Burt inquired politely.

Mike chuckled. "For weeks I have been trying to figure out what this funny feeling was. What a crack up. I'm *in love*. I'm in love—with my wife!"

Feeling happy and silly, he grinned at Burt.

Burt grinned back.

As Karen hung up her jacket in the hall closet at home, she felt something in the pocket. She reached in and brought out a folded slip of paper. Realizing Claudia must have placed it there, she opened it and read:

AN ELDER:

     STANDING IN A PLACE OF WISDOM WHERE PAST AND FUTURE ENTWINE,
     HE RESIDES IN BEAUTY, DEEP COMPASSION, AND ENDLESS GRATITUDE.
     HIS LIFE IS OVER. HIS LIFE IS FOR OTHERS.

For Good or Ill

"**H**I BURT. IT'S KAREN. IS CLAUDIA THERE?"

"Sure, Karen, just a minute."

Karen waited while Claudia came to the phone. It was Saturday evening and this was the first Saturday in over a month that she and Claudia had not spent together. She felt like she was going through withdrawal.

"Hello, dear. How are you?" Claudia asked in her lilting voice.

Instantly, Karen felt calmer. "Hi Claudia. I'm doing well, actually. I had my second trip to the beach today and I'm drinking lots of water. I even went horseback riding. But…I miss you." Karen felt embarrassed to admit it, but couldn't stop it from coming out.

"Ahhh," Claudia replied, "thank you. Tell me, dear. What do you get from spending time with me?"

"What do you mean?" Karen asked.

"Well, remember how I asked you what made you feel serene and strong and connected?"

"Yes."

"This is the opposite question. How does spending time with me make you feel?"

Karen felt uncomfortable but gave Claudia's question serious thought. "It makes me feel like I have some control in my life."

"Good," Claudia said. "Thanks for telling me. Is there anything else that makes you feel in control?"

After a moment, Karen said, "Strenuous exercise like running and aerobics. And yoga."

"That's great."

"Why do you ask?"

"I just wanted you to know you have a back up," Claudia replied cheerfully. After a pause, she added, "I would love to see you. How about tomorrow afternoon? What time is Mike getting home?"

"Oh, I don't think he'll be home until late. Tomorrow afternoon would be great. Do you want to meet somewhere?"

"How about you come over? Burt has a surprise for us."

"For *us?*" Karen didn't think she had heard right.

"That's what he said. How about two o'clock?"

"Great. Thanks Claudia. I'll see you then."

"You're welcome, dear. Thank you for telling me what you need."

Karen wondered about that last statement. Why would Claudia thank her for saying what she needed?

"Oh, Claudia, I have to tell you. Mike talked about dessert all the way home. He loved it."

"Oh, I'm glad. We think it's fun that way."

"That's what Mike said. That he hadn't had that much fun with dessert since he was a kid. You must have had an entire ice cream shop there. Hot fudge and hot caramel, whipped cream and nuts and cherries. Plus crushed Oreos and M&Ms, and the brownies and pecan pie!"

"Well, that way, Karen, everyone gets to make theirs just the way they like it. I believe in choice and the freedom to choose. I think it's important in life and especially important in dessert!"

"It was awesome, Claudia. I'll never forget it."

"You're welcome, Karen. It was my pleasure."

As Claudia prepared for Karen's arrival, Burt noticed that the tea time spread was more elaborate than usual. She normally set out cookies and, sometimes, some form of chocolate.

"Something special happening today?" he asked, indicating the cut flowers on the tray surrounded by fancy cookies, a bowl of raspberries, and fine china.

Claudia nodded. "This is our last session on the Stages of Development."

"Really? That happened quickly. So…after today…you're done with Karen?" He tried to sound casual.

Claudia looked at him squarely. "Just because I'm done with the Stages of Development, doesn't mean I'm done with Karen." She added, teasingly, "Mr. Nonchalant. Like you could fool me. I know you care how this goes from here."

Burt grinned because he loved it when Claudia teased him. Then he grew serious. "Yes, I do care. I care a great deal. So, are you going to let me in on your plan?"

"I don't have it all worked out yet. But, I'm getting close. I'll tell you when I know, I promise."

Burt pulled Claudia into his arms and squeezed her tightly. He felt her relax against his chest. She smelled like lavender. He leaned down and kissed the top of her head.

His voice coming out more gruff than usual, he said, "I'm glad you're not giving up, sweetheart."

Karen noticed the special treats on the tea tray. She assumed it was because today was Sunday. She had not learned any more about Claudia's spiritual connection since that one remark Burt had made while pointing at the clouds. But Claudia might be the kind of person who attended church on Sundays and made the rest of the day special.

Claudia led them to the dining room instead of the garden. Karen thought this must be because it was especially chilly today, which was unusual for Thanksgiving weekend in southern California.

"Did they have a special service today for Thanksgiving?" she ventured.

Claudia tilted her head. "A special service? Who, dear?"

"At church…" Karen coughed uncomfortably. "I assumed you went to church today."

Claudia chuckled. "I do seem like the type, don't I?"

Karen shook her head, hastily trying to find a retreat. "Well, no, not really."

"Then why did you assume I went to church?" Claudia persisted.

Karen gave up and decided she better just be honest. "A couple of weeks ago Burt told me…he told me about your boss."

"My boss?"

Karen pushed on. "Your *Boss*," she said, pointing up just like Burt did.

Karen could see the recognition register on Claudia's face. She must have seen Burt talking to her that day.

Claudia laughed lightly, and Karen felt relieved. "I had no idea he would reveal such a thing to you. I thought he was talking about the weather!"

Stick to the truth, Karen thought to herself. "I think he was trying to comfort me. I had just asked you to let me teach other women and…well, I'm sure you remember."

"What else did he tell you?" Claudia asked.

"He told me not to worry about upsetting you; that it wasn't what I had done. Something about a promise to your ancestors. I remember, especially, that he said it was the only area in your life where you suffer. Then he told me not to worry; that you had a promise to your family, but you would work it out with your boss."

Karen waited quietly while Claudia thought about this. She watched the older woman purse her lips and realized how fond she had become of all of Claudia's expressions, both her facial expressions and the quaint way in which she spoke.

Finally, Claudia said, "This question you asked about going to church is actually relevant to something I want to talk to you about. But let's save it for later. I have some other things I need to tell you, and then Burt has the surprise to show us. That's why we're sitting in here, actually. Burt is up to something in the garden and we're not allowed to even look out there until he says."

"Sounds interesting. The surprise, I mean." Karen added, "I didn't know you had something you wanted to work on—since we weren't planning on meeting this weekend."

"Well, I thought, since we are together, why not use the time for good?" Claudia responded.

"Okay, what do you have in mind?"

"Actually, if I were going to title today, I would call it 'for good or ill.' I want to talk to you about how you can use the information I have given you. How you can use it to help yourself and the men around you, and how you could use it to hurt them."

"Why would I want to hurt them?" Karen asked, surprised.

"Ahhh," Claudia responded, "that's what I have counted on you for."

"What?"

"That you have little desire to hurt men. Even when you were tearing your hair out over Mike's behavior in the Tunnel, you didn't react by wanting to punish him."

"Is that unusual?"

"Actually—and unfortunately—yes. Many women have a desire to punish men."

"Why would they want to do that?"

"Remember when we talked about how hard it is to admire and respect men?"

Karen nodded. It was just a week ago, wasn't it? Wow. Time flies when you're having fun. Or sex, she thought, and giggled.

She became serious. "Yes, I remember."

"Do you remember why you said it was hard to respect them?"

Karen knew Claudia was teasing her. "Yep! Because they screw up so much of the time."

"Exactly. Because women compare men to women—expecting them to do what a woman would do—it seems like men are misbehaving much of the time. And when someone is misbehaving, what must be done?"

Karen laughed as she saw it. "They must be punished!"

"Righto, chickadee."

Karen laughed again. Where does she get all these expressions?

"So, how do women punish men, Claudia?"

"Oh, boy. There is a topic worthy of hours of discussion, which we don't have today. Let's talk about how it backfires. Just as it would backfire if you tried to use the information I gave you against men."

This sounds serious, Karen thought, reaching into her purse and pulling out her pen and pad of paper. "Okay, I'm ready. Warn away."

"I may have told you that one of the things my ancestors have studied are the ways in which men react to women. There are things that women can do to bring out the best in men, and things we can do that bring out the worst. And, I mean, *worst*. A woman can turn a heroic, generous, protective provider into a raging beast or a completely withdrawn wimp."

"Can you give me an example, please? I'm not following."

Claudia nodded. "Sure. I want to talk about a couple of the main topics we've covered and what happens when you use that knowledge for good or ill.

"Let's start with the Stages of Development, since that is the main thing we have been working on, and understanding the stages is one of the keys to the kingdom. Using that information to understand men, you will have more compassion and understand better what you can ask men for. You'll be less disappointed and frustrated because you know what is fair to expect in each stage."

Karen nodded, interjecting, "Absolutely. I have experienced all of that. And it has been amazing."

"Good. Very good. But let me tell you what would happen if you used it against men. For example, let's say that you were single and having heard about Princes and the Tunnel, you decided you only wanted a King."

"How would that be bad? Isn't that a smart choice?"

Claudia pursed her lips. "That would all depend on what you wanted in your life. If what you wanted was to find a husband that fit a certain criteria—kind of like shopping for a washing machine—then you would know better what kind of product you were looking for. But that has a woman relating to a man like a *thing*. Each man is a separate, individual person. A person with a soul. A person with passions and dreams. A person who may be looking for someone with whom to share his life and himself. When the Stages of Development are used to treat men like things—a Knight-thing, or a Prince-thing or a King-thing—then we can't see *who they are*."

A light bulb went off for Karen. "You used the word 'see' again. I know you've said that we can use the Stages of Development to help us *see* why men do what they do. But they could also be used to *not see* who they are?"

Claudia was nodding vigorously. "Yes! You've got it. If a woman wants to build a partnership with a man, the Stages of Development can help her *see* the men who are ready for that and not be upset with them, or herself, when they are not. But if she starts judging men solely on their stage, that could prevent her from seeing the man who could be the right partner. Can I give you another example?"

Karen took up her pen again. She looked at Claudia expectantly.

"Another thing you have been working on is listening to men. By listening to them *with* interest and *with* an open mind, and *without* interruptions, you have seen how much men of all ages are able to express. This is another key to the kingdom. But the opportunity to express themselves is something that gives men power. Knowing this, you could intentionally do the opposite."

"What do you mean?" Karen asked.

Claudia took a sip of her tea. "Women have an unconscious fear of men being powerful. Since most women don't know how to deal with men directly, and effectively, they prefer for men to be weak and appear manageable. By interrupting a man, or by setting him up with no-win questions, a woman could prevent him from expressing himself and diminish his power."

"I know I did that with Mike. Not on purpose, of course. I just didn't know."

"When a man can't express himself, he is weaker or less powerful. He'll be much less productive. And he won't feel known or understood or appreciated by his partner, and that will kill his desire to provide for her."

"Gee, is that all?" Karen kidded.

"Actually, no," Claudia continued, "the relationship will suffer, too. There will be no real intimacy because intimacy comes from sharing our *selves*. And partnership will be unattainable."

"All just from not listening?" Karen asked in disbelief. But she did believe. She had experienced it. Fortunately, she was seeing it now from the vantage point of having recovered her intimacy and partnership with Mike. Just by listening in the way he, as a man, needed her to.

"What else do I need to watch out for?" Karen asked.

"It would be difficult to go through topic by topic. As long as you understand that emasculating and manipulating men always back-fires, you should be okay. Whenever men are less powerful, they are less powerful *for us*. Whenever we treat men like enemies, they have to respond to us like enemies. Instead of working to give us what we need and make us happy, they have to focus on protecting themselves from us."

Karen nodded, pretty sure she understood. "Claudia, is there some way to know that I'm hurting a man? I was disempowering Mike for a long time, but I didn't recognize it."

"You have to keep checking yourself."

"How do I check myself?"

"Excellent question. The way I was taught to check myself is by looking at the results. Am I empowered? Is he empowered? Or is one of us weakened? If we're both more alive or happy or able to pursue our dreams, then I'm probably on the right track."

Karen was writing furiously. Then a doubt crept in. "Claudia…honestly, are you telling me this because you are worried about what I am going to do with your information?"

She felt relieved when Claudia shook her head. "No, Karen. I'm telling you this mostly for me. That promise Burt spoke about…Years ago, my ancestors tried to teach women outside the family what we had learned about men. But the other women had not experienced partnerships with men. They naturally used their new knowledge to manipulate and diminish men. It was horrible. The men were weakened and the women got even less of what they needed. That is why we promised only to teach our own daughters.

"By teaching you, I have stepped outside my family's covenant. It is my responsibility to make sure you understand what will happen if you use this improperly."

Karen nodded. Then, like a dog that can't leave a bone, she asked, "Is that why you're afraid for me to teach anyone else?"

She watched to see if Claudia's eyes narrowed, the way they had that awful day a few weeks ago. But her eyes remained clear and open and fixed on Karen.

Claudia nodded. "Yes. I took a chance with you, partly out of intuition and partly out of the things you told me about your marriage. But I don't have a sure-fire way to predict when a woman would use our knowledge for good or for ill. Until I figure that out, I am reluctant to share this information."

Karen thought about the last statement. "Does that mean, if you can figure that out, you would like to teach more people?" she asked hopefully.

Claudia's eyes bored into hers and Karen felt herself being considered again, thoughtfully. It reminded her of their early conversations, when Claudia was sizing her up. She remained still and held Claudia's gaze, praying she wouldn't fail whatever test this might be.

Finally, Claudia said, "Earlier, you asked me about going to church. Because the Big Guy *is* my boss, that would be a fair assumption. But we converse privately and I rarely go to church. Most churches are a place to experience community. When I go to a church, I feel even more alone."

"Why?" Karen asked.

"Because there is no one like me, Karen. Any cousins I may have that pursued the same path were lost to me long ago. In my life, no one knows what I know about men, or what men have taught me about how priceless and powerful women are. No one *sees* what I see. When I watch women interact with men—at church or at the grocery store, or at the V.A. or the Chamber of Commerce—it is often painful for me. The sniping and bickering and bossing and disrespect feel like daggers to me. It hurts me to see men unappreciated. And it pains me that women don't understand their own value, that women don't know they are already loved by men. There is needless suffering and an enormous amount of power being lost and stolen that could be used to make life better for everyone.

"It is painful to watch it happen. And painful to be the only one who is seeing it."

Claudia paused and sipped her tea. She looked sad. Karen waited patiently, sensing there was more.

After a long moment, Claudia continued, "This is why I have made my decision about teaching you more of what I know."

"What have you decided?" Karen asked anxiously.

"I have decided not to teach you any more."

Karen gasped.

"…Until I find another student to teach with you."

"What?" Karen gasped again.

Claudia reached over and briefly took Karen's hand. "If I teach you all I know, I will be passing my curse on to you. It will ease my burden, but it won't be a kindness to you. If I teach only you, then you will have the problems I have. You will be alone with this precious information. But if I teach you and someone else, at least you will have each other. And then, when I am gone, or perhaps sooner, the two of you can figure out how to teach all the women that want to know."

Karen was stunned. The worst thing imaginable had suddenly turned into the best thing imaginable. She took a deep breath, which failed to calm her. Her mind was racing with the possibilities, compulsively outlining a curriculum of what she knew already. She completely ignored the significance of "when I'm gone."

"Do you have someone in mind for your second student?" Karen asked.

"Yes. But I don't know if she qualifies. It may take a little time to find out," Claudia replied.

"How much time?"

"I'm not sure. Maybe a few weeks. Maybe a few months. The right student is worth waiting for…like you."

Karen replied, "I wish we didn't have to wait at all! I'm anxious to learn what you know!"

Claudia chuckled. "You are going to have your hands full for awhile with what you've learned so far. You could take the next six months applying it and still not get to the bottom. There are all your students to understand, and their fathers, and the men at school. And, let's not forget, in all likelihood, the King will take his throne tonight. That is the beginning of a new life for you."

Karen gulped. "You think he'll come home a King?"

Claudia nodded. "Yes, I do. All the signs are there. He is ready. And, for a man on the verge, the Warrior weekend is a great facilitator."

"What do you mean by 'a new life' for me?" Karen asked, still anxious.

Claudia sipped her tea. "The biggest mistake women make when their husbands become Kings is not adapting. They think they are dealing with the same man they knew as a Prince. They will try to support and advise him like they always have. And they'll keep doing everything themselves. Our self-sufficiency is precious to us and it was honed while they worked all the time."

Karen picked up her pen again. She leaned forward in her chair, listening as if her life depended upon it. And she was sure it did.

"What should a woman do? What should I do?"

"You have not been aware of this, but you have been preparing for it ever since you met me."

"I have? How so?"

Claudia smiled. "We started with how to listen to men. You have been practicing that since the beginning. And done very well, I might add. Mike is going to need to be listened to, a lot. Without interruption and with an open mind. He will need you to be interested in discovering who he is now. If you are listening, he will express himself and you'll find out who you are married to. Never stop doing that. Don't ever be finished with discovering who he is."

She paused. "And you will need to receive and receive and receive. He will have much to give. You have already seen his generosity as you have inspired him with your love and compassion. As a King, his capacity for giving will be immense. You need to let him contribute to you. Let him make you happy."

Claudia sipped her tea. "He will need an enormous amount of appreciation. Not just a little here and there. A steady diet and a lot of it. Appreciating who he is and what he provides. Appreciating who you will get to be because of who he is. Notice and speak, notice and speak…Often.

"Lastly, the King needs a Queen. Keep doing the things that give you strength and serenity, and make you feel connected to Spirit. Don't give everything of yourself at work. Make sure you have greatness to give to Mike, too."

Claudia took a deep breath. Karen heard finality in it. "There," Claudia said, sitting back in her chair. "We're done."

Karen finished her notes and sat back as well. Tears welling up in her eyes, she looked through them at Claudia.

"Bless you, Claudia."

Burt was practically tripping over himself with excitement. He had the bench placed perfectly in the spot Claudia loved. It was finished. It was magnificent.

Whistling, he crossed the lawn and patio and entered the back of the house. He found the ladies in the dining room, embracing. He paused and waited politely, noting the tears on both of their cheeks. When they separated and both smiled up at him, he knew his timing was perfect.

"So, my angels. Are you ready for your surprise?" he asked with a grand gesture toward the back yard.

As they rose, he said, "Okay, follow me. And please keep your eyes down until we arrive at our destination."

He led them through the living room and out the French doors, down the steps, across the patio, past the path to his workshop and out onto the lawn to the far right corner of the garden. He watched and was gratified to see that they kept their eyes averted.

Stopping in front of the bench, he paused for effect and said, "My gift to both of you. Thank you for the inspiration you are together."

He watched as their eyes rose and took in the bench. He looked at Claudia, then Karen, as they were struck by what they saw. Their faces registered astonishment, then delight. He saw acceptance in Claudia first, as if she pulled his gift into her body and incorporated it into herself. She beamed at him and her eyes sparkled with love and admiration.

He watched Karen struggling, her body subtly squirming and shifting, her lovely face revealing an internal wrestling match. Finally, he saw her take a deep breath and let go a bit. Another deep breath and she smiled at him beautifully. Her eyes shining, she said, "It's magnificent, Burt."

Burt felt his chest swell. Exactly, he thought. He grinned at her in complete satisfaction.

Looking back at the mural of the Stages of Development—at his representation of their work—after a long moment he reached over and took Claudia's hand. He saw Claudia reach over and take Karen's hand.

The three of them stood in silent admiration of all their accomplishments.

New Beginnings

Mike took the long way home from San Diego, transitioning back to normal life through the solitude and enjoyment of cruising the back roads with the top down. As he entered the house, he looked around proprietarily. He nodded with satisfaction even as he noted improvements he now planned to make. He climbed the stairs quickly, knowing exactly what he wanted.

He found Karen tucked in bed, asleep with the light on, awaiting his return. God, she's beautiful, he thought. He brushed his teeth, undressed quickly, and crawled in beside her. As he lifted the covers, the pleasant smell of oranges and cloves emanated from her warm, luscious body. Snuggling close, he nuzzled her awake. Her eyes opened, she smiled at him and pulled him closer.

"Hi Honey, how was it?" she asked his neck sleepily.

"It was great, darlin'." He said in his cowboy drawl. "I'll tell you all about it tomorrow. Right now, what I'm hopin' for is some of your good lovin'."

He was delighted when she giggled and moved against him. He reached up and turned out the light.

Karen was proud of herself for being patient. It had been a busy morning for both of them, getting ready for work after four days off.

They agreed to a "date" that night, when Mike would tell her about his weekend.

Over dinner at home, Mike first asked about her weekend. She kept breathing and told him all about her trips to the beach, her horseback ride, her last session with Claudia, and Burt's bench. He was tickled that he had known about Burt's surprise ahead of time, and beamed while she talked about it. He was thrilled that Claudia had decided to keep teaching her, after she found another student.

"Any ideas who it will be?" he asked with a knowing smile.

"Why? Do you?" she asked, taking the bait.

He smiled again. "Something Burt said in the workshop. I think she's really hoping to teach Kimberlee."

After Karen thought about it, it made perfect sense. "Claudia said that she didn't know if the person she had in mind was qualified. I wonder what has to happen first," she said.

"Burt said something about Kimberlee opening her heart," Mike replied.

Another light bulb went on for Karen. "Remember the comment Kimberlee made about the table and chairs? That they were carved with roses? I thought the same thing for a long time, too. Then, suddenly, I saw the faces. It was like I was blind before. Like I just couldn't see such an extraordinary demonstration of love. Then, after falling in love with you again, I was open to it."

Mike smiled at her and took her hand. "I'm in love with you too, honey."

"You are?" she asked because she wanted to hear it once more.

"Yes, indeed I am." He paused. He added in his cowboy drawl, "But perhaps I am being a bit forward, ma'am. Please, allow me to introduce myself."

Karen's head tilted to the side. "Introduce yourself?"

"Yes. Introduce myself. Before you get any more mixed up with this cowboy, I want you to know exactly who I am."

Karen took a deep breath. Wow. She took another breath and consciously opened herself up to him.

"Okay. I would love to. Fire away, cowboy."

Mike shifted in his seat and sat up straighter. "This is what you need to know about me. First, I build *homes*. I hate building houses. I am going to create spaces in which people are going to love and laugh, and fight and play. I'm not going to build any more caverns or castles, no matter how much money they want to give me. Every room has got to be used every day, or I'm not building it."

Mike paused and Karen nodded her acceptance, although she couldn't tell if he was looking for that.

"I love cars. I love fast cars and old cars and red cars. I need a bigger garage."

Karen smiled.

"I love to travel. I want to revisit Zimbabwe. See if any of our old friends are still there. And see Australia and Europe and Alaska."

"Okay," she said.

"And I love you," he stated matter-of-factly and fell silent.

She could feel her eyes fill with tears and she blinked them back.

When she thought he was done, she matched his cowboy accent with her best imitation of a southern belle. "I'm pleased to meet you, Mr. Homes-not-Houses-Car-loving-Traveler."

Mike grinned at her and she knew she had done well. She smiled back.

"Oh, and one other thing," he said seriously while looking at her intently. Her heart skipped a beat.

"Yes?"

"I want to make babies. Lots of them. As many as we can have."

Karen gasped. A sob escaped suddenly from her chest. She gasped again. She could barely breathe.

Mike got up from his chair and came to her. She stood up and put her arms around his neck, looking up at him with tears of joy streaming down her face. His arms came around her waist and held her close.

Claudia smiled at Burt across the kitchen table. How many meals have we shared here? she wondered. It must be thousands.

She loved the easy rhythm they had. Anticipating the other's needs, moving in a dance together. The silences were as full and satisfying as their conversations.

Burt had been fairly floating since he revealed his newest work of art. After Karen had left yesterday, they had sat on the bench for more than an hour. Burt had told her all about each step of its creation. He explained the technique he had used to make the sun seem to glint off the Knight's sword. They had held hands and watched the glow of the sunset behind them reflect off the windows of the house and bathe the garden in rosy gold light.

Finishing her breakfast, Claudia took a sip of tea and sat back in the kitchen booth.

"I'm ready to tell you what I've come up with," she announced.

Burt set down his fork and sat back as well. He appeared calm, but his wrist was resting on the edge of the table and she could see his thumb and middle finger rubbing back and forth.

"Yes?" he asked smoothly.

"I told Karen yesterday that I don't want her to share my fate. I'm not going to teach her and leave her alone with this knowledge."

Burt looked steadily at her. His fingers paused.

"But I'm not willing to die with it, either. If there is one Karen, there must be two. Maybe there is a whole world of Karen's out there. Maybe there are millions of women who are ready for partnerships with men and just need to know how to understand them."

Burt nodded.

"But I don't know how to find all of them. And I don't think I have the time."

Burt reached across the table, took her hand and squeezed it.

"So I have decided to find one other student. Someone to be Karen's partner and companion in this knowledge. Then, it will be up to them to continue with others."

"Do you have any idea who this second student will be?"

Claudia nodded. "I am sure you know I am hoping it will be our granddaughter. And after all these years, I have finally figured out what I need to set aside the Covenant and teach Kimberlee everything."

"And what is that, sweetheart?" Burt asked gently.

Claudia squeezed his hand. She smiled with a touch of sadness and a touch of hope.

"I need her to ask."

Burt nodded his understanding and Claudia was comforted. She felt prepared to wait for Kimberlee to come to her. She hoped she wouldn't have to wait too long.

Ready for more?

"Every moment in our relationships with men is an opportunity to be understood or to be upset. To create freedom, better choices and more satisfaction in your relationships with men—and yourself— I invite you to participate in the Celebrating Men, Satisfying Women® weekend workshop for women."

—ALISON ARMSTRONG

What Graduates Say About
Celebrating Men, Satisfying Women®

"PAX Programs has transformed my life. It has opened up a world of men to me that I never saw. I now love and adore men. I see their amazing qualities and I am a happier person."

~ CAMILLE BARBER, Medical Sales, CA

"Knowing what men need and want to provide has given me the freedom to be who I am at my core. After 37 years of marriage I feel like I'm on my honeymoon."

~ KAREN REEDY, Eldercare Advisor, AZ

"Working with men was a challenge. We constantly struggled for power. At the workshop I learned what competition means to men and how to have it work for me, not against me. Now I love working with men and they love working with me!"

~ AYANNA MCKINLEY, Director of New Media, CA

"Since I took the workshop, I am more patient with my teenage son. We have a deeper understanding of each other and we're both happier."

~ ALICIA JOHNSON, Physician's Assistant, CA

"I feel more comfortable with myself – more rooted in my femininity, more at ease. I realize that I have always loved men. Understanding them better lets me feel safe living as their ally. Magic is happening!"

~ ELIANA URETSKY, Pilates Teacher & Garden Designer, CA

"I have taken many personal growth workshops and this one tops them all. I can really use this information and I am compelled to share it with all the women in my life."

~ MARGIT ELKEN, Educator & Artist, OR

"Before the workshop, I had not dated for years. After the workshop, I put an ad online and was dating 5 men by the end of the week. Now I have a boyfriend!"

~ DOMINEE MAURER, Graphic & Web Designer, CA

"I feel reborn! I feel confident about who I truly am and more accepting of what I have to offer. I am now in a life-long commitment to create peace and partnership in relationships."

~ HELEN DAVIS, Human Resources Manager, NJ

What Men Say About Graduates of *Celebrating Men, Satisfying Women®* and creator, Alison Armstrong

"I have lived with my beautiful wife, Louisa, for 30 years. She benefited greatly from the workshop, which impacted the quality of my life. Now that we've both taken PAX workshops, we have a better understanding of who we are and why we do what we do. We have tools and techniques to change our behavior when needed and are happier because of this. We now live in an environment filled with even greater appreciation, love and mutual respect."

~ KEVIN TWOHY, Relationship Educator, CA

"Since doing the workshop, my wife has developed a sixth sense about when and how it's safe to interrupt, how to listen intently and effectively, and how to be the best friend I've ever had. She also asks me for what she wants, tells me what she needs and is ecstatic and grateful when I deliver."

~ MICHAEL FRIEDLANDER, Web Marketer and Copywriter, NY

"After my wife Alicia took Celebrating Men, I noticed an energy shift in our home. We became more tolerant of our differences and began to enjoy spending time together even more. Our children noticed too. Our home is more peaceful."

~ DAMON JOHNSON, Educator, CA

"I've actually made an assignment out of one of Alison's DVD's for the women who work for me. We have noticed the difference in how we all relate to each other in and around the production and communication elements of the television show. And, Alison is the single highest ratings getter we've had on the show since it launched in June 2006."

~ DAVID SALINGER, VP Programming & Creative,
"View From the Bay," ABC7 KGO-TV, San Francisco, CA

"Being with women who have done the "Celebrating Men, Satisfying Women" workshop is to be deeply understood, lovingly cherished and completely listened to.

~ BILL ECAY, Business Owner / Advertising & Design, NY

MORE WORKSHOPS FROM PAX PROGRAMS

CELEBRATING WOMEN: REGARDING ECSTASY & POWER™
(aka The "Queen" Workshop)

- Learn to nurture your self-confidence and to be your best self – on purpose!
- Identify your needs and learn how to set up your life so that your needs are always met
- Expand your ability to receive and learn how to accept, decline and to negotiate graciously
- Find out what makes a woman worth dying for

CELEBRATING MEN & SEX™

- Learn the surprising things men value and what they need from sex
- Discover how emotional and intimate men want to be with women
- Learn how to honor your needs and become more self-expressed and satisfied
- Experience a new freedom to communicate about sex with your partner

CELEBRATING MEN & MARRIAGE™

- Examine all sides of marriage – what you need, what he needs and how to build a partnership through the challenges you share
- Discover how to quickly tell if a man can fulfill your needs without investing months of your time and energy
- Learn how men approach serious relationships versus casual dating and what qualifies a woman for marriage

UNDERSTANDING WOMEN: UNLOCK THE MYSTERY™
(A Co-Ed Workshop)

- Gain an in-depth understanding of the women in your life
- Learn how women think, act, speak, and listen and how to work with it instead of being frustrated by it
- Understand the mystery and importance of women's feelings
- Experience a toe-tingling "R" rated section on women's sexuality!

For details and to register, go to
UnderstandMen.com or call 1-800-418-9924

MAKING SENSE OF MEN™
a FREE Seminar for Women

LADIES:

Are you ever frustrated by men?
Are you ever confused by men?
Do you get mixed messages from men?

Come to *Making Sense of Men*™, a FREE seminar for women!
In only three hours, you could unlock the door to an entirely new way of relating to men. And, we'll hand you the key for free!

YOU WILL LEARN:

- How to tell when a man is really attracted to you – what he actually says and does.
- The 2 types of attraction men experience – the one that makes him cherish and adore you, and the one that will have him thinking only of how to get you into bed!
- Which qualities are the most attractive to men, and why they are essential to satisfying long-term relationships.
- What causes the "downward spiral" in relationships and how to have the "upward spiral" instead.
- How to decipher mixed messages with "MEN-Glish," the language of men.

RESERVE YOUR FREE SEATS NOW!
Call 1-800-418-9924 ext. 2
or go to
understandmen.com/reserve

PRODUCTS FROM PAX PROGRAMS

UNDERSTANDING WOMEN: UNLOCK THE MYSTERY™
Workshop-to-Go on DVD or CD

After more than a decade of helping women understand men, we have unraveled the complexities of women!

- Be surprised by the reason why women are compelled to multi-task
- Note which conversational details need to be remembered and which ones don't
- Discover the source of women's jealously and competitive behavior
- Learn how to repair hurt feelings and save you both from the "Rage Monster"

IN SYNC WITH THE OPPOSITE SEX
Workshop-to-Go on CD

- Unravel mixed messages you receive from the opposite sex
- Avoid coming on too strong
- Learn how to tell when someone is right for you or not
- Eliminate the pitfalls in pursuing the one you want
- Learn the benchmarks and timelines of dating and relationships, so you don't blow it
- Learn how predictable conflicts can create a structure for love, romance, and fulfillment

CELEBRATING LOVE
Audio Presentation on CD

Have You Loved and Lost?

- If you have given up on feeling love and intimacy in your relationship, figure out what went wrong and how you and your partner can fix it
- If you are fed up with your colleagues, boss or profession, gain new insight into what led you here and how to get back to satisfaction

Purchase products at **UnderstandMen.com or call 1-800-418-9924**

PRODUCTS FROM PAX PROGRAMS

THE AMAZING DEVELOPMENT OF MEN - 2ND EDITION
Audio Presentation on CD

- ❤ Discover the Stages of Development men go through from birth to seniority
- ❤ Determine what men live for and what they can't live without
- ❤ Learn how to avoid the tragic mistakes women make

- ❤ Discover what makes a man "ready" for relationships, marriage and children
- ❤ Learn how to respond well to the predictable changes in men instead of being stressed-out, left out or just left behind
- ❤ Understand that knowing the differences in these stages is critical for success in romantic relationships, raising sons and working effectively with men

THE AMAZING DEVELOPMENT OF MEN - 1ST EDITION
Audio Presentation on CD

- ❤ Discover the Stages of Development men go through from birth to seniority

- ❤ Learn what men need, can provide, and are unable to provide
- ❤ Understand everything from "workaholics" to "mid life crisis"
- ❤ Become more effective in choosing suitable mates
- ❤ Respond well to the changes in men – including fathers, sons, husbands, men at work and romantic interests

MAKING SENSE OF MEN: A WOMAN'S GUIDE TO A LIFETIME OF LOVE, CARE AND ATTENTION FROM ALL MEN
Paperback

- ❤ Learn why men pursue some women for sex and others for heart-felt relationships
- ❤ If your relationship started out great and then crashed and burned, learned why it happened, how to turn it around and how to prevent it from happening again

- ❤ Learn how to inspire generosity and attentiveness in all men

Purchase products at **UnderstandMen.com or call 1-800-418-9924**

About PAX Programs Incorporated: *Your Source for Understanding Men and Women*

PAX Programs Incorporated is in the business of educating women about men. PAX, the Latin word for "peace" is what you receive from participating in our workshops and using our products. Peace in your relationships with the opposite sex through:

PARTNERSHIP being on the same side or team.

ADORATION giving and receiving love, devotion, and respect.

XTASY experiencing joy and delight.

PAX is passionate about altering our society's culture by transforming how women relate to men. We provide extraordinary information with which women can profoundly affect their relationships with men of all ages and in all circumstances.

Company co-founder, Alison Armstrong, has studied men since 1991. The Celebrating Men® workshop series and catalog of products are the result of her insights. With a blend of humor, surprise and delight, PAX workshops lead you from confusion, frustration and resentment to understanding, appreciation and intimacy.

Our in-depth method allows you to see the opposite sex from a completely different perspective. You will gain a practical approach to working with the differences in men and women to create fulfilling and satisfying relationships – the kind that you have always dreamed were possible.

To learn more, visit our website at
Understandmen.com or call us at 1-800-418-9924

Notes